# The Smuggler's Bride

# The Smuggler's Bride

### By Rosalind Laker

DOUBLEDAY & COMPANY, INC.
Garden City, New York
1975

ISBN: 0-385-08997-X
Library of Congress Catalog Card Number 74–27638
Copyright © 1975 by Barbara Ovstedal
Printed in the United States of America

To the memory of Gerard Young,
who knew so much about Sussex smugglers
in days gone by.

# One

IT WAS QUIET in Perbroke Square. Harriette Mead, seated beside the driver of the cart hired to transport her trunk from the Tyburn Road tavern where she had alighted at the end of the coaching stage, noticed how the clop of the nag's hooves and the rumbling of the wheels echoed in the soft evening air.

She looked keenly at the tall terraced houses that were throwing back the sounds made by the humble conveyance. Built of russet brick, all had fine stone porticoes, gleaming brass knockers, and polished foot scrapers, with heavily pedimented windows looking out over the garden of trees, shrubs, and flowers, which lay like a lush green oasis in the middle of the square. The architecture was splendidly neoclassical, obviously designed to house families of considerable means, but due to the way London had grown and spread out in the latter half of the previous century, Perbroke Square on that late summer day in 1808 was no longer so fashionably sited as it had been in the past. But to Harriette, who had to work for her living, it was a matter of no importance.

Her fingers tightened involuntarily around the handle of the small valise which she held balanced on her lap. The cart was slowing its pace along the north side. Soon it would halt outside one of those imposing front doors and a new phase in her life would begin. Unaccountably, since the moment the jolting wheels had brought her within the confines of the square, a feeling of foreboding had settled like an ache in the pit of her stomach, almost as if she had unwittingly entered a trap, which was about to snap its bars shut around her.

Resolutely she dismissed the notion, telling herself it was natural to be nervous in those last few minutes before taking up a new post, even though she had reached the age of twenty and knew she had acquired some worldly poise.

"We're coming up to Number Seventeen, miss," the driver said, pointing with his whip. "Last but one in the row. See it? Next to the corner property."

Number Seventeen, Perbroke Square, was as bright and shining and well cared for in appearance as the rest of the houses, but its neighbor at the end of the terrace was a different matter. Alone out of all the other residences it had a neglected appearance, lacking paint and polish, its portico steps unscrubbed. Drawn up outside it was a carriage of contrasting elegance with burnished bodywork, four black horses with silken manes, and a coachman in gray livery. One of the grooms had been sent to hammer the knocker of the door of Number Eighteen and had failed to get a reply. As Harriette's driver dragged on the reins, bringing the bony nag to an obedient standstill outside her destination, she saw the groom give up his attempts at the neighboring house with a shrug of exasperation. He turned and hurried down the steps back to the carriage, where he spoke through the open window to the passenger within.

"There ain't no one at home, Mr. Sutcliffe. I be sure on't. I rung that bell twenty times at least, and banged the knocker more. But nothin' stirred."

A deep male voice, richly articulate, replied on a sigh. "Very well. Tell the coachman to drive on."

"Yes, sir!" The groom signaled to the coachman and sprang up onto the back of the carriage to take his place as it began to move.

Harriette, being on the side of the cart seat away from the pavement curb, waited for the horses and equipage to pass by before attempting a descent on two iron rungs to the ground, and she found herself looking straight through the open window at the gentleman inside. With his tall hat tilted slightly forward at a disconsolate angle that reflected his mood, he looked bored and disgruntled, although handsome in a black-browed, glowering way, and one gloved hand was bunched into a fist, which he pounded thoughtfully into the curved palm of the other. Unexpectedly, as he drew level with her, his gaze flicked in her direction and held hard. Taken by surprise, she met steadily that blatant stare of instantly aroused sexual interest that stayed clamped on her, fierce and dark and flashing, for those few seconds before the carriage bowled him past her and she was lost to his sight.

Within the seclusion of her bonnet brim she arched her brows in mild astonishment and a certain amount of self-reproof at the extraordinary quiver of response that had seared through her at that clash of glances. But as soon as her foot touched the cobbles her thoughts and attention became wholly concerned with the unloading of her baggage, and she hurried past the horse's head to reach the pavement, a slim, supple-waisted girl with gleaming dark gold hair, which gave a luminous look in brows and lashes to her wide hazel eyes. Her face was oval, her skin pearly over pretty bones, and her mouth full-lipped and firm.

She slowed her pace before reaching the portico steps, suddenly aware of being watched. Quickly she looked up at the residence where she was to be the new governess, expecting to see her future pupils peeping down at her, but there was nobody to be seen. Her gaze switched to the windows of the end house. On the first floor a silver-topped cane, reflecting a fiery flash of the setting sun above the housetops, had been holding aside the curtain for its owner to get a better view of her. But even as she turned her head toward it the curtain fell swinging back into place again. Harriette lowered her glance and went up the steps of Number Seventeen. So there had been someone at home there after all! In spite of Mr. Sutcliffe's groom getting no reply!

The driver had thumped her trunk down on the tiles in the portico, together with her hatbox and the valise, which he had taken from her hand. She paid him, added a small tip, which was all she could afford, and rang the doorbell.

A butler opened the door to her, and she was shown to a velvet-covered seat in the hall while two menservants carried in her belongings and bore them away up the stairs that curved gracefully out of sight. She had no more than a minute to wait before the butler returned and showed her into a drawing room with pale gray walls and white plasterwork.

Mrs. Elizabeth Warrington was reclining on a sofa, her light yellow hair cut short in the height of fashion with a frizz of curls on the forehead and a chignon at the back of her head. She was sharply feline, sleek and well rounded, obviously much cared for and waited upon, but her carefully painted face was stamped with a petulant expression as though she craved more out of life but was defeated by an innate laziness that she had no wish to overcome.

"Good evening, Miss Mead." With a languid sweep of her closed fan she indicated that Harriette should sit down opposite her. "You have had a long journey from Shropshire. Is this the first time you have been to London?"

"Yes, Mrs. Warrington. I welcomed this chance of obtaining employment in the capital."

"Your parents are dead, I believe. Have you any brothers or sisters?"

"I was an only child. To the best of my knowledge I have no relatives in all the world."

"When did you start teaching?"

"Soon after I was sixteen. Before that I nursed my father through a long illness—my mother died many years ago."

"What made you decide to be a governess instead of—well, entering domestic service, shall we say?" Mrs. Warrington smiled as though to sugar the barbed remark. Her teeth were small and ill shaped, and usually she did her best to hide them.

Harriette's expression did not change. "My father was a scholar," she explained patiently. "His many years of ill health impoverished him, but he was able to keep his books until the end, and it was his wish that I should put to good use all that he had taught me. I have not once regretted becoming a governess. I have found teaching to be truly rewarding."

Inwardly Mrs. Warrington mocked the remark. Rewarding indeed! Not on a monetary basis at thirteen pounds a year! It was not enough to keep a lady in parasols! But governesses were a race apart, expecting little out of life and receiving even less. Goodness knows, there had been a hodgepodge of them in and out of the house since she had informed Mr. Warrington some years ago that she had neither the time nor the inclination to teach their two daughters the three R's, and in any case it had become the mode to employ a governess to carry out such tedious tasks. Some of the young women employed—and some who had been not so young—had been barely literate themselves, but this Harriette Mead was different. She had been highly recommended by a family whose distinguished name Mrs. Warrington respected, which should have satisfied her, but somehow it did not. She was no longer sure that Harriette would fit submissively into the household, but it was difficult to discover exactly what it was about the girl that had irritated her from the moment she had walked into the room, neat, direct, and completely composed.

"In a few minutes you shall meet your pupils," Mrs. Warrington said. "As I told you in my letter, Phoebe, who is eleven, and Caroline, who is a year younger, are both exceptionally talented, but both have suffered from the incompetence of previous governesses. I trust you will do better."

Her tone suggested she had faint hope. She was still trying to pinpoint what it was about the new governess that aroused her hostility. Was it the girl's way of meeting her every glance with a clear, steady gaze that would not be forced down into a lowering of lashes in subjugation as was fitting to a person in her station in life? And that bonnet and high-waisted coat she was wearing! Castoffs, of course, but far too stylish—or was it that she *wore* them as if they were stylish? Ah! That was it! Harriette Mead gave herself airs! Praise for her work in the past had probably been too generous and it had gone to her head. There'd be none of that in this house. She should be humble and meek and polite at all times, or else at the first sign of trouble out she would go! A governess thrown out on the streets of London at a moment's notice would find herself in a rare pickle. So let Harriette Mead watch out!

Harriette was aware of being scrutinized, but did not suspect the reason. "Have you any other children, Mrs. Warrington?"

"My elder son is a lieutenant serving with the East Indian Bengal Infantry and has been in Babackpore for two years. Robert, my second child, is to join the same regiment as an ensign as soon as it can be arranged. Tell me what curriculum you have in mind for my daughters' schooling." When Harriette had given her a brief summary, she gave a nod. "It sounds well enough. Of course, I leave all such matters entirely to my husband, who decides what is best. Mr. Warrington will interview you upstairs in his study at nine o'clock, when he will make any alterations he thinks necessary to the educational course you have been accustomed to follow in your previous teaching. He is a strict disciplinarian and time-keeper. I advise you not to be a second late."

At this point the door opened and the two little girls came into the room. Harriette, rising eagerly to meet them, felt a pang of disappointment. Neither of them gave her an answering smile, but stared disdainfully at her. Phoebe, although she was the elder, was slightly shorter than her sister, as well as being a smaller edition of her mother with the same thin features and mass of corn-colored hair. Caroline, plumper, bigger-boned, no doubt favored her father, and she was the prettier, in spite of a certain darkness of expression.

"This is your new governess, Miss Mead," their mother said to them. "Show her how prettily young ladies of London can welcome a stranger into their midst."

Phoebe gave Caroline an almost imperceptible nudge. Both dipped in unnecessarily elaborate curtsies, murmuring, "How do you do, Miss Mead." Harriette, catching Mrs. Warrington's surprised reaction out of the corner of her eye, realized that a show fit for royalty had not been expected. But the little girls had had their backs toward their mother, who had not seen the mocking grimaces and thrust-out tongues that they had projected toward their new governess.

"I am very well, thank you, children," Harriette replied unblinkingly. "While waiting for you I have been telling your mama of the subjects with which I hope to engage your interest. I have just thought of another! Gargoyles! You shall take sketchbooks with you tomorrow, and we will explore the churches in the district until not a space on a page is left uncovered by drawings of amusing and often quite hideous faces!"

Phoebe and Caroline gave her savage glares. Had Harriette exclaimed at their ill manners or upbraided them in any way, they would have turned bland and innocent faces toward their mother, expressing complete bewilderment, thus establishing from the start that here was yet another hysterical female not fit to be in charge of them. No matter if their mother did suspect the truth, she would never side with a stranger against them, even when they were at fault, but often the bigger the lie the more receptive she proved to be toward it. Their father was another kettle of fish, and they kept out of his way as much as possible. Without doubt this new governess was going to prove to be a formidable adversary. She had neatly turned the tables on their carefully rehearsed and highly insulting behavior while at the same time punishing them for it under the unsuspecting nose of their own mother. Instinctively they drew back as though for protection, to stand one on each side of their parent, who placed her arms about their shoulders in the classic maternal pose.

"Such activities are admirable in moderation," Mrs. Warrington said to Harriette. "Not that I am against cultural pursuits, and an interest in church architecture is to be encouraged, but I do not want my daughters' heads stuffed with too many dry facts. However, I shall give instructions

7

that one of the carriages be brought to the door tomorrow morning at ten to convey you and your charges to the church or cathedral of your choice." She cupped the back of one hand gracefully in the palm of the other, her short spell of maternal concern over for the time being. "Now you shall see your room, Miss Mead. It is at the top of the house next to the schoolroom, which is most convenient. You will find it comfortable, I am sure, and you will have all the privacy you could possibly need."

Harriette soon saw the reason why it would be private, for her bedroom and the schoolroom, although plastered and painted and set with a fireplace in each, were under the eaves on the attic floor, which was approached by a steep and narrow flight of stairs. Unbuttoning her coat in the bedroom, she stood looking about her.

It was a large, bleak room with little furniture, the ceiling sharply sloping, but she had a winged upholstered chair to tuck herself into with a book, a sizable chest of drawers, a hanging cupboard, and two rugs that would spare her toes when she rose from the bed on winter mornings. Everything would look better when she had unpacked her trunk and taken out her belongings and hung up her pictures.

She put away her coat, removed her bonnet, and walked across to the window, loosening her soft, abundant hair by combing her fingers through it. Her room overlooked the long, rectangular garden at the back of the house, which ran parallel with its neighbors, culminating in coach houses at the end with extra loft accommodation for servants. In the deepening dusk she could make out the dark patches of flower beds, the glint of a pond, the careful arrangement of hedges and trees. By contrast the garden on the right-hand side, which belonged to the end house, was a wilderness that had not known a gardener's hand for many years.

Leaving the bedroom, she passed the head of the narrow staircase and went into the schoolroom, which—apart from some storerooms—took up the rest of the attic floor. From here the window looked out on the Square. Lighted windows had started to pattern the tall terraces, and to judge by the number of equipages drawing up on the west side, a soirée or a musical evening or some other social event was in full swing.

She turned her attention to the equipment of the school-room, lighting a lamp, which had now become necessary. There were two desks and a table for herself, some maps on the wall, and a globe, which she sent spinning with a touch of her finger while crossing to read the titles of the books on the shelves.

The clink of crockery made her straighten up, an open book in her hand. A footman had entered, bearing a tray on which there was a covered dish on a food warmer, a pot of tea, and a folded cloth. It was her supper.

"Are you eating in the schoolroom, miss?" he inquired. "The other governesses did. It's the only room up 'ere with a table."

She gave a nod. "Thank you. What is your name?"

"Jackson, miss," he said, spreading the cloth. He was obviously taciturn by nature and offered no more information, setting the table with quiet efficiency.

She leaned against the wall, watching him, her arms folded, the book dangling from one hand. There could be no lonelier status in life than that of governess, she thought with a rare plummeting of spirits. Unaccepted in the servants' hall with its strict hierarchy that put her above its entire class, and compelled to stay out of the way of the family at all times, she always occupied a kind of hinterland in the house, and in this case it was the attic. Previously she had had pupils of whom she had grown fond, even when they had been lazy or had proved to be a challenge, making her use all her initiative to capture their interest and improve their work. Phoebe and Caroline had shown themselves to be spoiled and difficult, making it plain that they didn't intend to cooperate, although she suspected that the older child was the ringleader and that Caroline, if encouraged to assert herself, might eventually become more amenable. In any case there was going to be a struggle, but no work was ever done without discipline, whether it came firmly from the teacher in charge or was self-imposed by the pupils themselves. Her schoolroom had never been a shambles, and she did not intend to have one now.

The supper was well cooked and, hungry from her long journey, she ate every scrap of food and drank the teapot dry. Afterward it was getting toward the time when she was due to see Mr. Warrington in his study, and she went back into her bedroom to brush her hair and give a last tidying touch to her appearance.

She had the brush in her hand when there came the sound of slow and muffled footsteps. Turning her head, she looked toward the half-open door in some surprise, thinking that someone had come up unheard to the schoolroom. A rumbling shout echoed somewhere, and this time she swung about sharply to look toward the wall that divided her room from the corresponding room in the end house next door. It was from there that both sounds had come. The echoing effect suggested that the attic in Number Eighteen had not been paneled or furnished, for there had been a hollow ring to it. As she stood there listening there came another shout, farther away and less resounding, and then there was silence.

Thoughtfully she brushed her hair. The occupants of the next house seemed decidedly odd, not answering their front door and shouting about in the attic. But she had no time to wonder about them now. Her fob watch told her that she must finish her toilet quickly and start looking for Mr. Warrington's study somewhere on the second floor.

She was not looking forward to meeting Mr. Warrington, who was a stern enough character for his own wife to warn her not to be late in attending him, and she went purposefully but somewhat slowly down the narrow stairs from the attic floor. The next flight was wider with a polished sweep of handrail, and Harriette, continuing down at the same steady pace, suddenly realized that there was a thumping tread of footsteps descending the corresponding flight of stairs in the end house. She paused. By chance, whoever it was on the other side of the thick wall paused too. She had the uncanny feeling that the person standing there was listening too. Had the clack of her heels on the wooden stairs penetrated that dividing wall? Surely not, for her step was light enough.

She took two more steps down, and then stiffened. There had come an echoing blunder of movement down the flight on the other side! An absurd sense of panic seized her. For a few ridiculous moments she was tempted to snatch off her shoes and speed down the rest of the stairs in her stocking feet, but common sense prevailed, and she told herself that somebody was attempting to play a joke on her. But it didn't seem like a joke. Determinedly she swept down to the next floor and tried not to think that it was like running away.

On the landing she looked about hesitantly, wondering which of the doors belonged to Mr. Warrington's study. Somehow she had expected to find it waiting and ajar. Mrs. Warrington had said that it was facing the stairs and had been no more explicit than that. She tapped on one door and then another without result. But the third time a male voice abruptly bade her enter.

She entered a plainly furnished room. Too late she realized it was a dressing room. In shirt sleeves and waistcoat, his hips narrow in slender trousers of palest gray, a young man stood with his back toward her, getting ready to go out to some evening function and giving the final touch to the fold of a white linen stock at his throat before the looking glass. His reflected eyes met hers under brows raised and amused; her own gaze was startled and dismayed.

"A thousand pardons, sir!" she gasped. She would have withdrawn hastily, but he halted her.

"Wait!" he demanded, turning to take up his coat and slip it on with a swish of silk lining. "Who are you, pray?"

"The new governess!" She was anxious to make her escape. "I was looking for Mr. Warrington!"

"But I am he."

She could tell he was laughing at her, but not unkindly, although he was enjoying her confusion. "Then you must be

Mr. Robert Warrington," she said, guessing his identity. "It is your father I'm seeking, so if you'll excuse me—"

"What made you think you might find him here?" He came strolling toward her. His face was well assembled with a straight, thin nose, nostrils strongly curved, his skin clear, smooth, and burnished, his teeth very white and even, his chin hard and square.

"I thought this room might be his study."

He reached out and gripped the edge of the half-open door, grinning at her. "It would be—on the floor below."

"How foolish of me!" She was intensely annoyed with herself for having let the strange incident on the stairs distract her from her bearings. "I've only been in the house a couple of hours and I haven't yet become accustomed to my surroundings." His arm was barring her way. "If you will excuse me—"

"What's your name?"

"Harriette Mead."

"I'd heard some mention of another governess coming, but that was all. It's a pretty name. It suits you well, ma'am." He seemed intent on delaying her. "Where are you from?"

She told him briefly. "Now I must go—"

He ignored the agitated little flurry of her hand. "My brother and I had a tutor until we went away to school. Unlike the governesses who have taught my young sisters from time to time, he remained for all those early years, in spite of our attempts to make him tire of impounding knowledge into us." His chin lifted as he chuckled. "Perhaps tutors are more resilient than governesses. Admittedly they have a cane to enforce their authority, which ensures them some respect. What of you, Miss Mead? Are you resilient? Or are you likely to be driven away like the others?"

The corners of her mouth responded in a smile. "I intend to stay, Mr. Robert," she said firmly. "Do not doubt that!"

"You relieve my anxiety, Miss Mead." There was a depth of meaning in his words, the tilt of a promise, the charm of challenge. He inclined his head in a bow, showing that he was willing at last to let her go.

With a little start she realized his arm no longer barred her way. She shot him an uncertain glance before hastening off down the stairs. He watched her out of sight before closing the door, and there was a look of satisfaction on his face. Turning back to the looking glass, he stood buttoning up his coat, but he was not thinking about his appearance, his thoughts lingering on Harriette. He had been afraid that the weeks left in London before going abroad would prove to be tedious and constricted, his father being excessively mean in diverting the greater part of his miserable allowance, which had never been sufficient, into the compulsory settling of some wretched debts, but things had changed. A pleasant little diversion had loomed up unexpectedly under the same roof. In the meantime, a late evening at his club awaited him. There at least he could be in amiable company and away from his father's sour disapproval, but at all costs he must avoid the gaming tables or else, remembering his recent run of ill luck, which was causing him to be turfed out of England and into the army, he would have no money left at all with which to entertain and amuse the little governess who had stepped so unexpectedly into his life.

Harriette, slightly flushed and in an unusual fluster at knowing she must be late, located the study without any further difficulty. She found Mr. Warrington, a grim, red-faced man, awaiting her with his gold watch cradled in the palm of his hand. He gave her no greeting, but looked deliberately from her to his watch, and then at the clock on the chimney piece.

"You are six minutes late, Miss Mead. Six minutes late, I said. It will not do. Will not do. Eh? Do you think it will do?"

She did not know if he expected her to make some excuse, but she had no intention of doing that. She had been advised not to be tardy, and the fault was entirely her own, for she could have left Robert earlier if her true inclination had not been to dally longer in his company.

"I shall not be late again, sir," she said determinedly, and meant it.

"Hmm." He studied her speculatively from under his bushy

brows, his chin drawn back into fleshy folds, his heavy jowl indented by the points of his high collar. "I trust not, young woman. I trust not. Time and tide, y'know." His broad thumb closed his watch with a snap, and he returned it to his waistcoat pocket. "Sit down. Take that chair where I can see you. That's right. You've met my daughters, I hear."

"Yes, sir."

He clasped his hands behind his back, and with his feet set apart he rocked his portly frame. "Bright as buttons and pretty as pictures. I do not deny it. You will not deny it. But that is not enough. Oh, dear, no. Not by any manner of means. Their education must be completed, Miss Mead. Completed, I say." His staccato speech served to emphasize his complete satisfaction with every statement that he made, a reflection of conceit, a complete self-assurance that sprang from a dogmatic authority, which Harriette suspected came very close to tyranny. "You are here to do that," he continued, "and punctuality is the secret. On time at the desk. On time for expeditions—I hear that a sketching outing has been arranged for tomorrow. Excellent. That is excellent. Be sure that there is an allotted space of time for each drawing and no more. Let the work of art be completed within the number of minutes set, or demand to know the reason why. Work to the clock!" He shot a finger up into the air. "The clock!"

"I can only say that I shall do my best to keep to a carefully thought out routine," she said.

He waved aside with a contemptuous gesture the idea that it was any responsibility of hers to arrange the routine. "I have prepared the syllabus, which you must follow. I believe I know best the kind of education suitable for young girls of my daughters' place in society." He went to a side table and picked up a closely written sheet of paper, which he handed to her. "Read it through carefully. You will find other instructions for you to observe."

In bewilderment she bent her head over the paper and read it through. She was to be given no free rein in the choice of subjects or in the timing of the lessons, the length of which was set down. The school day was to be long. Eight o'clock in the morning until five in the afternoon six days a week, although an hour's walk was allowed once a day when the weather was fine. No wonder Phoebe and Caroline had greeted her with such hostility! The only respite from work came between the departure of one governess and the arrival of the next. She saw with relief that one day a month was to be spent in visiting a place of interest, such as the Tower, the Royal Academy, or the Montague House museum at Bloomsbury, but she guessed that her pupils would not soon forgive her for turning their one day out this month into a punishment!

Her exasperation mounted at the petty rules and restrictions that were to govern each day. The insistence on discipline, with the children being kept quiet and mannerly at all times, made it easy to guess that her predecessors had not been entirely successful in this respect, and Mr. Warrington was obviously a man who did not like his life disrupted or upset in any way. With an inward sigh she lowered the paper and looked up at him.

"I have never subjected any of my previous pupils to such a grueling daily grind," she said, hoping to reason with him. "In my experience children learn better when they are allowed some relaxation. I must respectfully remind you that I shall be teaching two little girls—not hardy students used to studying for long hours on end."

Mr. Warrington's mouth tightened ominously. He did not take kindly to criticism of any sort, however mildly expressed. "And I will remind you, Miss Mead, that you have been teaching the children of country squires. Shropshire ways are not London ways! No, indeed! Indeed not! That is why I am taking you on trial. On trial! What is good enough for another man's children is not necessarily good enough for mine! No, not for mine! Do you understand?"

Harriette gripped the polished ends of the chair arms. "You made no mention of a trial period when you sent for me, sir!" she exclaimed, thinking of the long and expensive journey she had made from her native county to reach London.

"Better all round, don't you see!" he answered pontifically. "No dismissal to cause you embarrassment when applying for another post if you should prove unsatisfactory, and no payment on mine, your board and lodging being more than enough remuneration in that case. More than enough!"

Harriette sat white and speechless. The man was miserly as well as bigoted! Had she anywhere else to go she would not have tolerated such an imposition, but she had nowhere, and he knew it. And neither did she have anyone to whom she could turn for advice.

She found her voice and the words came out on a deeply anxious note. "How long a trial did you have in mind?"

"Three months." He did not appear to notice how her face became stricken at such a long period of uncertainty, and he continued without pause. "I am not an unreasonable man. Not unreasonable at all. Should you not wish to remain under those circumstances I would not dream of asking you to leave my house at this late hour. You may remain until morning. Early morning, of course. Well, what is it to be? Shall you stay, Miss Mead? Eh?"

She had no choice. The small favor he was inclined to grant her gave no time to make other plans. With a sickening lurch of despair she recalled how, with happy confidence, she had drawn on her meager savings to buy new books and a small loom to interest her new pupils in weaving, believing it to have lost too much ground over the years to embroidery and petit point, and it was a craft at which ladies had once excelled. She had also purchased a coat for the first time in four years and had made two new gowns, which she was certain she would need. There were two pairs of shoes too, and sundry other small items for the new venture into the alien surroundings of a great city. Even her special economy in retrimming an old bonnet with ribbons and relining the brim with a scrap of new silk now seemed a totally unnecessary extravagance grown out of all proportion.

She could not leave Number Seventeen Perbroke Square. Her feeling of foreboding had not been wrong after all. The cynical thought flitted through her mind that it was a great pity that she had not been afflicted by it before leaving the county that she knew and where it would not have been so frightening to be faced with the threat of unemployment. Whatever happened she *must* survive the three months in spite of anything that might occur. And why not? She compressed her lips determinedly. She could teach and she knew how to encourage and inspire. Her confidence came flooding back, and she was amazed that she had let any foolish doubts assail her. Together she and the girls would overcome the barriers that impeded progress. It was not impossible. She would find some way to lighten their yoke. It was a challenge to her ability as a teacher and she would meet it!

Purposefully she rose to her feet and faced her employer. "I will stay, Mr. Warrington."

Then it occurred to her that it was the second time within an hour that she had reaffirmed on a distinctly fervent note her intention of remaining with the Warrington household. It was almost as though she felt the need to convince herself as well as others that all would go well. Was she more nervous about it than she cared to admit, even to herself? Was she making a brave show? Whistling in the dark perhaps?

She went back up to the attic rooms at a much slower pace than when she had descended. Passing the dressing room door, she felt a twinge of disappointment at seeing the door closed and no streak of lamplight showing beneath it. Secretly she had hoped that Robert might wait to waylay her again, although she knew it was nonsense to place any importance on his apparent interest in her. She had met attempts at flirtation before from the older sons in other houses where she had taught or stayed on holiday at county seats with her pupils, but she had rebuffed them from the start, determined not to endanger her situation in any way. The mistress of a household invariably closed her eyes to the indiscretions of her menfolk when they became involved with young females belowstairs, turning out at a moment's notice any maidservant unfortunate enough to become pregnant, but a governess was a different matter.

Higher up the social scale, usually coming from a respectable family background, an attractive, ladylike young governess could arouse thoughts of marriage in the minds of those older sons destined for far more advantageous and profitable matches. Such romances were nipped firmly in the bud, and the governess would be sent on her way with adequate testimonials, but all doors slammed on any false hopes that she might have dared to entertain. Harriette had long since resolved never to find herself entangled in such an ignominious state of affairs. It had meant keeping a close guard on her heart, which she knew to be vulnerable, long denied the joyful release of meeting love with love.

With a heavy sigh, she pushed open the bedroom door and went in. Perhaps she had been luckier than she had realized in the past, able to shield herself from any emotional commitments simply because she had never met anyone quite like Robert before. Her feelings were in an odd turmoil, as though her blood were racing through her body at twice its normal rate. Thinking the matter over, it seemed to her that she had not felt the same person since she had received that burning stare from the stranger in the carriage, and she concluded that every small thing that had happened since she had first ridden into Perbroke Square was responsible for making her nerves throb so near the surface.

Lost in thought, she sat down on the edge of the bed and removed one shoe and then the other. She must not lose her head if Robert should look at her again with such mischief in his blue eyes. She smiled to herself, leaning her arms on her lap and dangling the shoes from her fingers. His eyes *were* blue. Blue as summer skies. Blue as Wedgwood. Deeper than speedwell. And his thin-lipped, mobile mouth was splendidly shaped and exciting. What would it be like to be kissed by such a mouth?

One of the shoes swung off her finger and dropped with a

clatter to the floor, bringing her back to reality. It was dangerous to entertain such daydreams. She must be on her guard against any kind of interest taking root and blossoming into something more serious. There was no doubt she was ripe for love. It was behind the restlessness that had brought her to London. She had turned down a most honorable offer of marriage from a widower, whom she had liked but could not love, and it had resulted in an intense longing to take wing and fly free to meet an unknown destiny. But she had flown straight into an attic cage. To be trapped more securely by circumstances than she had ever been before!

She bent to pick up the shoe and placed it with the other neatly by the wall, as though by taking excessive care in a few mundane tasks she might keep all thoughts of Robert at bay. Her reticule was lying on the chest of drawers, and she took out the key of her trunk to start unpacking. Her possessions, neatly folded, lay revealed as she lifted the lid. It did not take her long to empty the trunk. Her gowns she hung away in the cupboard with her coat, and her petticoats and other underwear she folded away in the drawers. It took her a little longer to decide exactly where to hang her three small paintings, originals by a Shropshire artist purchased by her father long before she was born, which gave her familiar views of the green, rain-misted countryside that was so dear to her. On a shelf she placed the two porcelain figurines, which she had saved from the home that had been sold long since; then in readiness for the day when she could find some flowers on a nature ramble she put out on the chest of drawers the white enameled vase of Bristol glass which she had bought quite inexpensively in a market one day.

She stood back and regarded the room. Nothing could make it cozy, but it did look more homelike than it had before. How tired she was! It would be good to get to bed.

For a while the rocking of the coach on that two-day journey over rutted roads to London was still with her, but eventually she slipped blissfully into a sound and dreamless sleep. She would not have awakened until morning if the quilt had not slipped from the bed, taking the blanket with it, and leaving her half covered by the patched and mended sheet.

Sleepily she sat up and reached out to the chair at her bed-side for her fob watch, and she turned its face toward the moonlight. Peering at it closely, she saw that it was only half past two o'clock.

Shivering, she took a shawl from the back of the chair and put it about her shoulders. On bare feet she hurried across to the window to close it. With her hand on the latch to draw it toward her, she happened to glance down, and her gaze became riveted to the neighboring garden of Number Eighteen, which lay laced by moonlight. She was convinced some-one had moved down there in the black shadows. Was there a prowler at large? Crime was rife in London, and she had heard that it was not uncommon for violence to be done on unsuspecting people in their beds before a house was stripped of all its valuables.

Not daring to move, she stood there, holding her breath, ready to rush away down the stairs and raise the alarm should the need come about. Then she frowned in puzzlement. A bowed, square-shouldered figure in a cloak had moved into sight, and he was plodding slowly along with the aid of a stick on which he leaned heavily at every difficult step. She could see his moon shadow lying in his wake. Even as she watched, he turned about with a lurch and began slowly to retrace his steps in the attitude of someone pondering a deep problem—or taking necessary and leisurely exercise to ease stiffened and painful joints.

She could not see his face. It was hidden by his tricorne hat, which was much misshapen and of a style worn in these days only by liveried coachmen, or else by elderly men who clung—either through a lack of means or a dislike of the new cocked hats and top hats—to a dead fashion, often continuing to powder their hair as they had done in their younger days, instead of leaving the custom to footmen and other such menservants. Was this coachman or householder who paced the garden? It was impossible to tell. What an hour to take exercise! And in such a jungle of overgrown trees and tangled undergrowth! But his relaxed attitude was completely law-abiding, and she no longer had any fears that he was an intruder with no right to be there. Indeed, his rather disreputable appearance was certainly in keeping with the state of the garden and no doubt with the interior of the house itself.

She shivered again, which reminded her that she was getting colder every minute and the nocturnal constitutional of the man was no concern of hers. Hastily she pulled the window closed, but it needed an extra tug to make the latch drop home. It made a small sound in the quiet night, but the man heard it. He stumbled back quickly under the cover of the trees, and although the branches hid him from her view she knew that he must have looked up and seen the pale oval of her face at the window.

Quickly she bounded back into her bed, her feet ice-cold from the bare boards, and she drew the rearranged covers up over her head to shut out the night and all that lurked in it. Before long she was asleep again.

# Two

IN THE MORNING Harriette, standing by the window while she tied her bonnet strings, decided it would not be hard to imagine she had dreamed the whole thing about the old man in the moonlight. But she knew it had been real, although the garden that lay parallel to that of the Warringtons looked as wild and untended as though no human foot had trodden its overgrown paths for years. Perhaps he hadn't been human. Her eyebrows went up in amusement at the eerie thought, and she decided it would not be hard to imagine that either!

Turning away from the window, she picked up a cloth bag by its handle, in which she had put sketchbooks and drawing materials, and went downstairs, where both children awaited her in their outdoor clothes. She greeted them with a smile.

"Good morning, Phoebe. Good morning, Caroline."

"Good morning, Miss Mead," they replied in a glum chorus, and fell in behind her to go out to the waiting carriage. Harriette had noticed that Phoebe looked sullen, but Caroline looked only resigned, as if it was not the first time she had had to pay the penalty of letting her sister involve her in some mischief. Harriette, although she intended to keep them extremely hard at work on the outing as a deterrent to future bad behavior, had hopes of turning the day to advantage by pointing out items and sights of interest, which could be followed up on expeditions in more agreeable circumstances.

She had read many books about London's history and architecture in preparation for her coming, and she thought a particularly old church in Southwark by the river would provide the sketching opportunities she was looking for that day. She gave the name of it to the coachman before taking her seat in the carriage, the two little girls opposite her, their backs to the horses.

She had been looking forward to her first real glimpse of London by day, but the two children bickered and squabbled so ferociously that she was forced to make one sit on either side of her to keep them apart, and she had no chance to give her attention to the passing streets.

Folding stools had been brought, and while these were being set up in the churchyard by the groom Harriette led the girls around the outside of the ancient church, telling them something about medieval architecture and the points to look for in a Gothic building. They listened with undisguised boredom, their mood becoming increasingly rebellious. When she took them into the church to see the hammer-beam roof and the intricately carved foliage they showed no interest, and shuffled their feet noisily, making a few other people present stare toward them disapprovingly. When Harriette reproved them in a sharp whisper they clacked their heels instead, obviously determined to behave in the most irritating manner possible for the whole time.

Outside again they argued over where to sit and which stool was the best. When finally settled they broke their pieces of charcoal, dropped their sketchbooks, giggled helplessly, and fell off their stools. But Harriette was a match for them, and with a determination that equaled and finally overcame theirs she kept them at their work.

Gradually Caroline, who had some artistic ability, began to take an interest in what she was doing, and she shrugged off in annoyance Phoebe's attempts to make her ruin her sketch paper by smudging it.

"Leave me alone and get on with your own work, Phoebe," she snapped irritably. Then a glint of malevolence showed in her eyes. "I'm drawing a gargoyle that looks exactly like you!"

Phoebe glanced up quickly at the gargoyle in question, and her expression became outraged. It was popeyed with a long nose and pointed ears, its hideous and pointed-toothed grimace trickling water from a gutter. Without a second's hesitation she wrenched Caroline's bonnet down over her eyes, making her squeal with fury. In the ensuing scrap the drawing was crumpled, but Harriette, after drying the child's tears and sending Phoebe to work at a safe distance away, managed to smooth the paper out again and it showed that no real damage had been done.

When the carriage returned to Perbroke Square, Caroline gathered up her day's work protectively, making sure of keeping it out of her sister's way. She was first out of the carriage when it came to a halt, not waiting for the groom to lower the step, but jumping down and dashing up into the portico, where she huddled herself into a corner, clutching her drawings as though in hiding.

Phoebe, a smirk on her face, alighted with a swaggering nonchalance and sauntered up to the door. "Baby!" she taunted her sister. "*I'm* not afraid of anyone!"

"Was he at the window?" Caroline inquired nervously. "Did he see me?"

"Mr. Hardware sees everybody who goes by," Phoebe retorted. "I shall spit up at his eye one day!"

"Phoebe!" Harriette reproved sharply, ringing the doorbell for admittance. "That was not polite! Of whom were you speaking in such an ill-mannered tone?"

"The monster who lives at Number Eighteen!" Phoebe answered in a shouting voice, as though intending to be overheard, and she peeped around the pillar at the end house. Caroline went wide-eyed at such bravado and held her drawings up over her face, overcome by her sister's daring. Phoebe, seeing this action, laughed mockingly. "Watch out, Carrie! He'll come through the wall that divides our house from his one dark night when you can't sleep, and he'll bite off your head and crack it between his old teeth like a nut!"

Caroline gave a shrill scream of terror at her sister's words.

24

Jackson had opened the door and she bolted through it, her drawings scattering in all directions. Sobbing noisily, she flew up the stairs and vanished from sight. Somewhere a door slammed shut.

"Well!" Harriette took the gathered up papers that Jackson had handed to her, and she looked sternly at Phoebe. "That was a cruel and heartless thing to say! No wonder your sister is frightened of your neighbor if you make up such scaring tales! The fact that—Mr. Hardware, was it?—walks with a stick is no cause for stupid, mindless mockery! I'm extremely displeased with you! It comes as a final disgrace after your appalling behavior today!"

Phoebe paid no attention to Harriette's reprimand, her narrow eyes sharply curious. "How do you know he walks with a stick? Did you see him in the garden next door during the night? I never have, but I know our other governesses sometimes saw him out there talking to himself, and the servants have spotted him from the coach house at the end of our garden." She came close to Harriette, her expression spitefully eager. "Did you see his face?"

"No, I did not," Harriette replied, regretting her slip of the tongue in mentioning that she had seen him. She had no wish to discuss Mr. Hardware with Phoebe. "Give me your sketches, such as they are. I'll take them up to the school-room with me."

Phoebe passed them over automatically, her mind still intent on the topic that she found so absorbing. "He never goes out of the front door by night or day! Not even to get into a coach. And he only walks in the garden after dark. Mama believes him to be horribly disfigured—I overheard her talking about him once." She lowered her voice in a whisper of delighted horror. "Perhaps he hasn't a face at all!"

"Whether he has or has not is not a matter to be gossiped about," Harriette said, patting the sketches into a tidy pile against the crook of her arm and moving toward the stairs. She was resolved never to stare out again at the unfortunate man. Perhaps he had been badly scarred by the pox, which could do terrible damage to the face, or had suffered some war wound that he felt made him impossible to look upon. That he was old she had no doubt at all, her mind having registered his sagging stature, but he was powerful still, for there had been no frailty in the hand that had swung the stick and leaned on it.

Phoebe came trotting up behind her, reluctant to drop the subject. "Mr. Hardware moved in next door five years ago —and after dark so that nobody saw him. He lives there alone, except for a housekeeper, who is a miserable old crone at least a hundred years old. We see her sometimes, but she never speaks—not that she would to us, of course, but not even to our servants, who have tried to find out about her master—"

"Enough!" Harriette came to a halt halfway up the stairs, and she hammered a fist on the handrail, looking furiously over her shoulder at Phoebe. "I'm tired of your prattle! I will hear no more of it! The best thing you can do is to apologize to your sister for trying to frighten her! And think about your neighbor with some compassion instead of with such spiteful inquisitiveness!"

Phoebe looked taken aback, astonished that her salacious interest was not shared. But she recovered herself almost at once, and she hissed through her teeth after Harriette, who had continued up the flight. "You wait! That's all! Why do you think the other governesses left? It wasn't only because Papa found them incompetent and sent them packing! Every one of them was scared of being alone in the attics!"

Harriette swung around and looked down at the girl. "Why should that be?" she demanded, forced to challenge such a statement.

Phoebe's malicious gaze was unflinching. "They soon guessed the truth, that's why! Mr. Hardware is mad! Fit for old Bedlam! That's why he turns night into day and bellows and shouts and stamps about! There's no other explanation!"

"I'm prepared to believe he's a little odd in his ways, particularly if he suffers from some cruel disfigurement," Harriette conceded, "but why should that make anyone afraid of being on her own at the top of the house?" She made her point coolly. "According to you, he shuns all company and most certainly he wouldn't as much as look over the garden wall!"

Phoebe grinned triumphantly. "Not over the garden wall! But he could come charging *through* the house wall! The governesses have all lived in fear that one night they'd find the bricks smashed away, and that terrible madman coming through from the next-door attic to murder them with his bare hands!"

Harriette smiled grimly. "You have a vivid imagination, Phoebe. Fortunately I'm not easily alarmed, but I feel sorry for anyone who allowed such foolish improbabilities to scare them."

She turned away once more. Phoebe, undaunted, took a few running steps up and shouted after her.

"You'll end up as scared as the rest of them! Haven't you wondered why no maidservants are accommodated in the attic? It's because they wouldn't stay there." Her voice took on a savage edge of vindictiveness. "Mama says that governesses are ten a penny, but good servants on moderate wages are hard to come by. She doesn't intend to lose those that she has, or else Papa would have to pay the new ones more money these days, and then he would insist on making do with one servant less. So there, Miss Mead-ten-a-penny!"

With this final taunt the girl scurried away, giggling on the high note that borders on hysteria, not at all sure that she had not gone too far. Harriette did not pursue her, although anger had heightened her color. Ten a penny! The insult stung all the more for the amount of truth in it. There were far too many governesses for the positions available, for parents naturally put the education of their sons before all else, believing that their daughters did not need to have very much money—if any!—spent on their learning. It sounded as though Phoebe had repeated her mother's words most accurately, and it was certainly unusual not to find domestic staff occupying part of the attic. She herself had never been given

27

a room at the top of a house before, but then the other houses where she had worked had all been much larger with sprawling wings, having no need to cram a schoolroom under the eaves.

"How did you get on today?"

Harriette looked up with a jolt of pleasure at the sound of Robert's voice. He was leaning his arms on the banister rail where it curved widely to follow the next flight up. She smiled back at him and relaxed, letting all problems fly from her in the enjoyable surprise of this unexpected encounter. He must have just come in himself, for he had his hat and cane in his hand, and his hair, which he wore in the fashionably short windswept style, had been slightly disarranged by that same element. She thought him the most endearing young man she had ever met, bewitched by his smile, his twinkling eyes.

"It went much as I'd expected," she answered, happy to talk to him about anything, even his spoiled and difficult sisters. "We did get quite an amount of work done in the end."

He made a grimace of sympathetic understanding. "I can guess what that means. Did Phoebe and Caroline behave abominably?"

She hesitated. "They were not on their best behavior, I can tell you that! But I have hopes that things will get better as we go along. I think I imparted some knowledge. I also discovered that Caroline has an eye for perspective and can draw remarkably well."

"Indeed? I'd like to see some of her sketches."

Harriette began to rustle through the papers. "There's a particularly good one of part of the church roof—"

"Later. I'd like to see it later."

She raised her head again and looked at him, holding the drawings closer to her. "Later?" she echoed.

He nodded, holding her eyes. "Perhaps you could spare me an hour after dinner. I can come up to the schoolroom."

She knew then that he cared nothing for his sister's artistic efforts. It was a pretext. He wanted to further their acquaintanceship, and her heart quickened at the thought. It would be fun to acquiesce and be granted a full sixty minutes in his company to talk some more, laugh, and get to know him. But common sense, which could make life so mundane, prevailed.

"I think not." Her voice gave nothing away. "Tomorrow lessons start in earnest, and I want to get everything ready this evening."

He was unrebuffed. "Another time then."

She made to go past him. "I cannot say. I expect to be kept extremely busy."

He barred her way. "Come now. You're not going to be as busy as all that. Tell me when I can see my dear little sister's drawings."

He seemed to delight in making gentle fun of her. She chose her answer carefully. "I suggest Wednesday afternoon next week. The children will be having a painting lesson. A still life. A vase, some fruit, and a few flowers. You can watch Caroline at work with watercolors."

The look he gave her was decidedly quizzical. "That is out of the question. How can we talk freely to each other when others are in the room, Harriette?"

She was as startled by his bold use of her Christian name as she was by his casting aside of all pretense, but she did not lose her composure. "We meet in the presence of others or not at all."

"We're alone now," he pointed out.

She shook her head, smiling. "Passing on the stairs is of no account. Good day, Mr. Warring—"

He took hold of her by the arm, his face serious, all teasing gone. "You're too young and pretty to be shut up in the top of the house away from everything! Why should your life revolve around a schoolroom!"

"That is why I am here," she reminded him.

"Let me show you London!" he urged. "Do you like music? There is the opera, as well as many fine concerts to attend. You will want to visit Vauxhall Gardens, but you cannot go unescorted. I will take you there! We can go boating on the river if you would like that. London is full of the most amusing diversions."

She could not suppress the longing in her face. He was offering her a London she had thought only to view from a distance, seeing others flock to such entertainments. But it was impossible. It would lead to all sorts of complications. She bit her lip regretfully, her eyes dark with disappointment.

"It would not be wise. You must see why. Now I must get on with all I have to do." She hurried from him to prevent any further argument.

"Harriette!" he exclaimed impatiently. "Don't go!"

She did not pause or look back. It would be all too easy to change her mind, and she must not let that happen.

She busied herself in the schoolroom before her supper and after it, filling inkwells, cutting a supply of quill nibs, hanging up maps, setting out books, and preparing the lessons. It was quite late when she went into her bedroom, but being far from sleepy she settled herself in the cushioned chair to stitch for a while by candlelight. It was the hem of her coat that she had to mend, having caught her heel in it when getting out of the carriage.

She was absorbed in what she was doing, her thoughts drifting over the day and lingering on Robert as he stood there on the stairs, when there came a thump from the corresponding attic room in the house next door. But she paid it no attention, fastening off the thread, and pressing the finished work with the ball of her hand.

Then such a tremendous crash came against that intervening wall that she sprang to her feet with a gasp, her coat, the needle, and what was left of the thread falling together from her lap to the floor. She stared at the wall, not moving. The blow had been as loud as if the eccentric Mr. Hardware had wielded a blacksmith's hammer against it, and for a few tense moments she awaited a further onslaught, half expecting the bricks to go flying in all directions under a cloud of dust and leaving a space large enough for someone to come through. But another blow did not follow, and inwardly she mocked her own twinge of near panic, reminding herself that if ever such an unlikely event happened she would have plenty of time to flee to safety. Perhaps some of the other governesses had been much older than she was and less agile. Poor bewildered, unhappy women if this had been the kind of shock that they had been subjected to!

She stooped down and gathered up her coat again, which she placed over the arm of the chair, but she could see no sign of the needle. Taking the candle, she knelt on the floor and searched for it. No bright glint caught her eye, and she felt about with careful fingertips. When she followed the grain of one floorboard it suddenly vibrated to the distant thump of Mr. Hardware's heavy footstep, and she snatched her hand away, sitting back on her heels.

He was shouting now in a thunderous voice, but it was impossible to distinguish the words and she was thankful for it, not wanting to eavesdrop. Nobody was answering him, and she realized that he must either be talking to himself or addressing someone whom he imagined he could see. It was an eerie thought, and she did not welcome it, wishing it had not occurred to her.

She rose to her feet and, with the candle in her hand, went across to the wall. Carefully she examined it for some sign of cracking, but the bricks had been plastered well in their time and the only splits that showed were superficial, fine as hairs and dark with age. That did not suggest that a hammer of any kind had been used on the wall from the other side. Then what, she puzzled, was it that had fallen with such force against it?

She made up her mind to question Mrs. Warrington about Mr. Hardware at the first opportunity, deciding that she must cut through Phoebe's ridiculous tales and find out the true facts, not out of idle curiosity, but in order to find the patience to endure such disturbances.

It was impossible to sleep until long after midnight. Mr.

Hardware paced slowly up and down, the thud of his stick accompanying the dragging thump of his foot as he swung his weight forward. Sometimes he bellowed at the top of his voice, and at others he muttered at length on a low rumbling note. Finally he clumped away downstairs, and in the stillness that followed she caught the echo of his erratic descent, which made her realize that he had not been keeping pace with her on the corresponding stairs the previous evening. A man so handicapped would need all his efforts not to fall. She supposed he had gone down to take his nightly stroll in the cheerless garden, but she had no intention of looking out to see.

The following morning Harriette caught a glimpse of Mr. Hardware's housekeeper going by with a shopping basket on her arm. She was a tiny, wizened little woman with an unhealthy, yellowish pallor. She was dressed in shabby clothes, all her hair pushed into a grubby mob cap on which she had tied a wide-brimmed black hat. But three more days went past before Harriette had a chance to talk to Mrs. Warrington about Mr. Hardware.

"I am not acquainted with the occupant at Number Eighteen," Mrs. Warrington said disdainfully. She was in the middle of a fitting for a new gown in her boudoir and she spoke to Harriette as she rotated for the dressmaker, who was busy with the hem. "Neither do I wish to be, I hasten to add! I believe him to be an excessively vulgar person, judging by the strange hours he keeps and the way he shouts at his housekeeper, who is fortunate enough to be deaf and probably hears only half of it."

"But he is on his own when he rampages about after dark," Harriette said. "Not a night has gone by since I came without a noisy disturbance of some kind. Once it was ten minutes, but other times it has been up to two hours or more." The previous night she had heard him sobbing. Wild tearing sobs as though he beat his breast in some insupportable grief. She had sat up in bed with a stricken face, having no choice but to listen to the harrowing sounds.

Mrs. Warrington was more interested in the draping of her skirt than Harriette's comment for the next few minutes. "A little more fullness to the right, I think. No! Not as much as that! Ah! That is better." She turned her head somewhat reluctantly to take up the conversation with Harriette again, still keeping a wary eye on what the dressmaker was doing. "Mm? What did you say? Oh, yes. The noise. You are not the first governess to mention it, not by any manner of means. Mr. Warrington called once on Mr. Hardware to make a complaint, but he got no further than the old housekeeper at the door, who was extremely rude to him."

"Didn't Mr. Hardware receive him?"

"Dear me, no. She swore that he was not at home—and not in a genteel manner, but with abuse that Mr. Warrington should dare to call! After that my husband wrote a letter politely requesting less noise, but it was never acknowledged, and one day that dreadful old woman threw the torn-up pieces all over our steps when she went past! I wonder sometimes if she gave it to Mr. Hardware, or whether she ripped it up herself. It is quite a madhouse in there. Fortunately the paneled walls keep the noise away from the family apartments and we hear nothing at all, but I am aware that the attic is exposed to the full inconvenience of it, and this was why Mr. Warrington made his call. But nothing more can be done. I live in hope that one morning we shall wake up and find that Mr. Hardware has moved again in the night as suddenly and mysteriously as he came. In the meantime I am afraid you must suffer the din. That is all there is to it."

"Does Mr. Hardware have no visitors at all?"

"To my knowledge only one person has ever crossed the threshold since he came, and that is a lawyer whom my husband knows by his unsavory reputation. Mr. Bellamy-Jones is notorious for his sharp dealings and his defense of rogues and scallywags able to pay well. I shudder to think what hideous disfigurement it is that keeps Mr. Hardware from mixing in society and avoiding the light of day. What is more, he sits for hours behind the curtains watching all that goes on in the Square, so do not lift your eyes when you enter or leave this house. Ignore his existence in every possible way. That is an order. Do not disobey me."

Harriette, closing the boudoir door behind her, felt she had really learned nothing more about Mr. Hardware, but she would obey Mrs. Warrington and try to ignore his presence as much as possible, however difficult it might prove to be.

"Are you avoiding me?" Robert stood facing her across the landing. He looked put out and offended.

"Not at all."

"I have seen no sign of you since we met on the stairs the day after you came."

"I do not have a spare minute."

"Surely in the evenings we could meet!"

"There is nothing more to say on that topic!" she cried in a voice of anxious insistence.

"I disagree! Why should we not talk now? Lessons are over for the day, are they not?"

She was relieved to have a ready excuse. "Not quite. Your sisters are getting their outdoor clothes on to go with me into the garden in the middle of the Square. They are trying to see how many different leaves they can collect to press in their nature-study books."

He spoke with emphatic bitterness. "It seems that I must join Phoebe and Caroline at their lessons after all if I am to make any claim on your time!"

But that was an idle taunt, for his sisters came clattering out of their room at that moment, and he flung one angry look in their direction and departed hastily. Harriette realized he had quarreled with her. The resulting hurt was hard to bear.

In the garden the girls ran about picking up the leaves, arguing about who would have the biggest variety, and Harriette sat on a stone seat, watching them. What was the matter with her? Why was she moping like this? Robert was as spoiled as his sisters, angry when thwarted, losing his temper when he could not get his own way. He knew as well as she did that if either of his parents even suspected his interest in her she would be sent packing. It was unfair of him to tempt her with promises of romantic evenings spent at the exciting places that he had mentioned. But oh how she longed to go to them with him!

Somewhere in the Square somebody had started to bang a door knocker with a force that demanded attention, but she did not trouble to turn her head, her view hampered by the leafy arbor in which she sat. Caroline came dancing up to her.

"I've found some beautiful leaves! Look at all the different greens!"

Harriette thought it tied up with the child's artistic ability that she should look first for color. "Nature has an infinite variety of hues," she said with a smiling nod.

Phoebe came strutting over to look with contempt at her sister's collection. "Silly! You have lots from the same trees. Not like me! I have gathered twenty-four different ones."

"It is no matter," Harriette said, rising to her feet. "Both collections will be of interest for different reasons. It is time to return to the house or you will be late for your daily half an hour with your mama."

The children ran ahead of her across the road, which was bare of traffic, although a horse was looped by its reins to a hitching post near Mr. Hardware's house. It was the rider who had dismounted to demand admittance—and in vain to judge by his impatient jerking of the bell, his knocking having brought no result. But her thoughts were concentrated on Robert. She wondered if he was still indoors or if he had gone out. Better not to see him, of course, but the hostility in his eyes haunted her and she felt choked inwardly.

Benedict Sutcliffe, giving the bell a final pull, swung about at the sound of the two little girls running up the steps of the portico next door, and he looked to see if they were accompanied by an adult whom he could question. Stepping onto the curb was a slender young woman in a russet-colored coat, and although the brim of her bonnet hid her face from him, for her head was bowed as though in thought, he recognized her instantly. With a swirl of his coattails he sprang down the steps of Number Eighteen and strode across to meet her.

"Your pardon, ma'am." He swept off his hat and stood bareheaded. "I beg leave to address you."

She looked up sharply. He saw the preoccupied look flash from her face, but doubted that she remembered him. "Sir?" she said uncertainly.

But she did know him. And she was aware that he was gazing at her again with the same burning interest. His strong dark voice matched his appearance, which at close quarters was even more overwhelmingly physical with his brooding, magnetic looks than when he had been at a safe distance in the carriage. He was taller than she had realized and broadly built, not as young as she had first thought, but about thirty-two or -three. His face was powerful with jutting cheekbones and a square brow and chin, the nose high-bridged and straight, the nostrils winged, and the long mouth oddly enhanced by a deep indentation in the middle of the lower lip, which was an open indication of an intensely sensual nature.

"Could you by any chance tell me if your neighbor is in residence?" he inquired politely. "I have called several times without getting to see him."

"Mr. Hardware is always at home, I am told," she replied, "but I understand that he receives no visitors."

"The devil take him!" he exploded, glancing angrily over his shoulder at the house. Then he apologized for his outburst. "Forgive me, ma'am. I am afraid my patience has worn extremely thin. Even my letters are ignored."

"His housekeeper does answer the door sometimes. She is deaf. Perhaps she has not heard you."

"She may or may not have heard me," he stated grimly, "but she certainly knew of my arrival today. I saw the curtains twitch. The first time I called she opened the door an inch, and when I gave my name and asked to see her master she slammed it shut again and shot the bolt home!"

"Don't be disheartened. It seems that everybody receives the same hostile reception. You have not been singled out."

He raised an eyebrow in exasperated bewilderment. "Does nobody get past the old harridan at the door?"

"Only Mr. Hardware's lawyer."

"Ah, yes. I know the fellow. He was equally wily about Hardware's whereabouts, refusing to give me the address. I had to engage other help to discover it. One might be tempted to think that Hardware feared the coming of the bailiffs and for that reason keeps his door locked against all comers."

This suggestion interested Harriette. It was certainly the first sound reason she had heard that could explain the man's torment. "That is a possibility."

"Oh, no, it is not! Hardware owns other property and some acres of the richest farmland in Sussex. It cannot be a thin purse that makes him so cautious of visitors."

"You are well acquainted with Mr. Hardware then?"

"I have never met him, but since his lawyer excuses himself from the authority of dealing with an important matter that needs Hardware's attention, I do not intend to give up until I come face to face with him. Then I—" He broke off, for Phoebe, her expression petulant, had come out of the house again and stood on the top step to address Harriette in a voice of whining complaint.

"Miss Mead! We are waiting for you! Shall we take the leaves up to the schoolroom or not?"

Harriette colored, realizing that she had spent far too long talking to this stranger. "I'm coming, Phoebe." The child swung around and went back indoors.

He gave a bow. "Forgive me. I have detained you too long. Good day, and my thanks to you, ma'am."

"Good day, sir." She hurried into the house and found not only the children waiting for her but their father too.

"Are you in the habit of gossiping with gentlemen in the street and neglecting your duty toward your charges, Miss Mead?" he demanded in a voice of thunder. "Your duty, I say! What has become of it?"

"I could not ignore a courteous request for information," Harriette replied stiffly.

"Information? What kind of information? Did he ask to be directed to some street or address? Or did he wish to dally away the time of day with you?"

She could not help feeling that Mr. Sutcliffe had prolonged the little conversation, not that she had been aware of it at the time, but that was nothing to do with Mr. Warrington. "He wanted to know if Mr. Hardware was at home."

"What?" Mr. Warrington blew through his nostrils. "I believe my wife has told you most firmly to ignore the existence of anyone in the house at the end of this row of residences! Most firmly! That also means not discussing that particular person with anybody you may meet under my roof or anywhere else!"

"I shall remember that in future," Harriette replied with dignity, angry that her employer should be reprimanding her in front of the children, who were listening with malicious enjoyment.

"I trust you will! This is London! London, I say. Not your local countryside! Respectable young women do not engage in conversation with strangers in the street. Remember that, Miss Mead. That is what you must do. Remember it."

Accompanying the children up to the schoolroom, Harriette thought she was not likely to forget it, or that particular day. First of all there had been trouble with Robert, followed by an unwanted meeting with Mr. Sutcliffe, who had the experienced man's way of looking at a woman that made her well aware of the thoughts running through his head, and finally the unhappy scene with Mr. Warrington. Phoebe and Caroline were sniggering together. She hoped her discipline had not been too much undermined. The best thing to do was to use it as an example of the need to learn as much as possible, pointing out that even adults must adapt to new surroundings as quickly as they could, and that she herself had learned that passing the time of day in a country village was different from an encounter in the streets of London.

In the morning she found a red rose on her schoolroom table. It was wet with dew from the garden, and she knew that Robert must have slipped up and put it there before the house was astir. She held it by the stem and rested the bloom on the palm of her other hand, gazing at it with a great uplifting of her heart. He regretted his sharp words to her and had sought in this touching way to make amends. Slowly she raised the perfumed head and inhaled its sweet fragrance, her eyes closing. Never had she received anything that had given her more pleasure.

It was standing in her Bristol-glass vase when the children arrived to take their places at their desks. Phoebe did not notice it, but during the morning Caroline went to put her nose to it and sniff the perfume appreciatively.

"Isn't this a lovely rose!"

Harriette came and stood by her, touching a petal gently with her fingertips. "It is indeed. I am going to press and keep it."

Phoebe looked up from her copybook. "Why? There's nothing special about that sort of rose. They grow in everyone's garden."

Harriette smiled. "This rose made me feel happy as soon as I saw it, and I think that is a good reason to preserve it." She looked at Caroline. "Don't you agree?"

Caroline beamed. "Oh, I do. May I help you press it? I have that heavy book of stories for good children, which would weigh it down."

Phoebe snorted derisively. "That is the best use for it as far as you are concerned, Carrie! Nobody could call you good unless they were as mad as Mr. Hardware!"

Harriette rapped the desk sharply. "After what was said yesterday you know as well as I do that we do not refer to our neighbor under any circumstances. I have learned my lesson, and you must learn yours. Now carry on with your work. Go back to your place, Caroline. I want that page of copy writing finished before the lesson ends."

Work was resumed, but although her two pupils kept their eyes on their books Harriette found that her own gaze drifted continually toward the rose. She watched the dew dry on it, and when the sun touched it to ruby highlights and velvet depths she carefully moved it into the shadow again in order that it should not fade quickly. Throughout the day its haunting perfume drifted across to her. She kept smiling to herself, blissfully content.

# *Three*

IN THE DAYS THAT FOLLOWED Harriette saw Robert several times, but never once was she without the company of the children. He used them as an excuse to speak to her and somehow managed to hold his own private conversation with her through the casual chatting that took place. On their first meeting after the giving of the rose she had greeted him with such a spontaneously joyful smile, showing she had accepted the gift in the spirit in which it had been given, that his glum expression had been dashed away, his eyes lighting up in incredulous delight. He then laughed and talked so animatedly with her and his sisters that Nurse Galloway, who had looked after the girls since they were infants, came by chance across the hall and gave all four of them a disapproving frown. Robert, who had never liked her, made such a droll face after her retreating back that Phoebe and Caroline became helpless with giggles, and Harriette, smiling herself, hastily ushered them back upstairs to the schoolroom.

She found herself going about the house with her hopes on tiptoe. Any door that opened could bring him out to speak to her, any corner might be the one around which she would come across him. When she took the allotted hour for a walk with the children she was sometimes rewarded with the sight of him riding his black mare out of the Square, off on some appointment of his own. And on one delightful afternoon he actually joined them, having caught them up on foot, and never had time flown more quickly.

She refused to consider the possibility that she was falling in love with him. It was so against her resolution to avoid all such complications that she tucked it away at the back of her mind. Even when she lay sleepless, the covers over her ears in a vain attempt to keep the echoing sounds of Mr. Hardware's terrible grief or his defiant blunderings out, for that was how they appeared to her, she thought only of Robert's smiles, the special glances that he gave her, the moment when his hand had accidentally brushed against hers—or had it been accidental?—and she would go over yet again all the words they had exchanged, even when it had merely been a comment on the weather.

By the time she had been in the Warrington household for a month Harriette was able to confirm in her own record book that her first impression of her pupils' ability had not been wrong. From the start it had been obvious to her that Phoebe was the brighter of the two, quick to learn when she could be persuaded to put her mind to it, but careless and often slovenly in her work, which was more a gesture of defiance than a lack of concentration. On the other hand, Caroline, although her reading was poor and her arithmetic abysmal, was neat in everything she did, her sewing stitches always even, her painting, in which she took a keen interest, carried out with painstaking care. But she excelled in the verbal telling of a story, which Harriette encouraged, hoping it would eventually prove to be an aid to the child when setting anything down on paper, which was always a slow and laborious task for her.

One afternoon with a little time to spare before lessons ended, Harriette suggested that a story from Caroline would round off the day. The child sat on a stool beside Harriette's table and told a particularly gripping tale of a dragon trapped in a castle and unable to get out. Harriette noticed how the child's face became quite pale with excitement, her eyes taking on a glazed, faraway look as if she could really see the scaly, fork-tailed creature, breathing smoke and fire, whose desperate efforts to get free she was describing.

*42*

"Well done," Harriette said when the story came to an end. "Tomorrow it would be interesting to see how much of it you could write down. Try to remember the exciting way you told it this afternoon."

"Yes, Miss Mead."

Harriette glanced at the schoolroom clock. "My goodness! We have quite forgotten the time while listening to that splendid tale! You should have gone downstairs fifteen minutes ago."

Caroline turned to her desk to pack up her books. Phoebe, having closed the lid on hers, regarded her sister jealously.

"Who thinks dragons are real then?" she taunted under her breath in a singsong voice.

Caroline slammed her books down again. "They are! They are!" she cried, her face flaring crimson. "I know they are!"

"Stupid baby! There haven't been dragons for hundreds and hundreds of years! They were all killed off by King Arthur's knights and St. George and some of the other saints."

"That's not true!" Caroline's eyes watered on the brink of angry tears. "Some must have escaped! It stands to reason!"

"They'd have been found. How could they hide away roaring and spitting fire as they did!"

"There were caves, weren't there! In mountainsides and under cliffs where the sea kept men at bay! That's what happened! And there they stayed until a fearsome master came along looking for one to guard his property!"

Phoebe sniggered mockingly. "Someone like Mr. Hardware perhaps? Who believes that there's a dragon in Mr. Hardware's house?"

Caroline flew for her. Too late, Harriette rushed forward, but they fell to the floor, scratching and kicking and biting each other, screaming and shouting in temper. They rolled against a chair, which went crashing over.

"Stop! Stop!" Harriette cried fiercely, trying to pull them apart. "Phoebe! Caroline!"

They paid no heed, although Phoebe, getting the worst of

it, became intent on flight, struggling to her feet. Caroline, clinging to her like a limpet, tore some hair from her head, which brought forth an ear-splitting shriek. With one supreme effort Harriette seized them by the shoulders and wrenched them apart, holding each at arm's length on either side of her, both equally disheveled.

"What is happening here?" demanded Mrs. Warrington's shocked voice from the doorway.

Phoebe took immediate advantage of her mother's unexpected arrival on the scene. She darted across to bury her face against her, wailing noisily. "Carrie attacked me, Mama! Oh! Oh! Oh! She scratched my face and hurt me!"

A familiar sullen look settled on Caroline's face. "I was provoked, Mama," she said defensively.

Mrs. Warrington pushed Phoebe from her, almost in distaste. Her maternal feelings did not run deep. She liked children to be neat and clean and polite, handsome if possible; otherwise she preferred not to see them. When they had been babies they had been put into her arms only in rosebud condition, wrapped in snowy shawls, and she dandled them for a little while, but had soon become bored. Her resentment at the display of temper which she had just been in time to witness was directed wholly against the governess who had allowed it to happen.

"Miss Mead! I have never seen such a disgraceful exhibition in all my life! Is this the way you take charge of my daughters? I am greatly shocked! Mr. Warrington shall be informed as soon as he returns! To think I came all the way up here, believing some absorbing lesson was still in progress, and instead I find a scene out of Bedlam!" She flapped a disapproving hand at her offspring as though finding the sight of them too much to bear. "Go down to your room immediately and get Nurse to wash your scratches and help you tidy yourselves up. You have both torn your dresses! What frights you look! I do not wish to have you near me again today!"

The children departed hastily, thankful to escape, although they could expect a similar upbraiding for the state they were in from Nurse Galloway in whose company they had long since refrained from attempting physical violence on each other, for she had mean ways of punishing them. Mrs. Warrington, without another word to Harriette, followed them, but keeping at a distance, which emphasized the disgrace they were in.

Alone in the schoolroom Harriette slowly set about tidying up, her actions detached and automatic. Picking up the chair and putting it on its legs again, she became aware that she was trembling. She was certain Mr. Warrington would dismiss her, and then what would she do? Destitution stared her in the face. The little money she had would not keep her long in the cheapest of lodgings, and some she would have to spend on advertising for another post. But it would take time to get replies, and what if she had to journey out of London to see a prospective employer? If it was a matter of a few miles she would have to walk there and send for her trunk afterward—if she could find somewhere to leave it where it would not be rifled or stolen. But if any great distance was involved she could not afford fares, not even if she rode on a wagon instead of taking an outside seat on a stage as she had when coming to London. Her thoughts were in a turmoil.

When everything was back in place again she sank down on her chair at the table to wait for the summons to Mr. Warrington's study. Nothing like this had ever happened to her before. She watched the hands of the clock move around one hour and then two. Mr. Warrington must be late home. Still she waited.

It grew dark. With a shaking hand she lighted a candle. Jackson was off duty and a maidservant brought her supper, which was a clear soup and a large piece of pigeon pie with floury potatoes. It looked appetizing enough, but she knew she would not be able to eat anything.

"I'm not hungry, Sarah," she said. "It's pointless to leave it."

"Oh, miss! Ain't you well?" The maid studied her with a frown of concern.

She gave a deep nod. "I'm well. I just don't feel like eating. Tell me, is Mr. Warrington at home yet?"

"Yes, miss. He came in half an hour ago."

So he was dining first. Harriette looked at the clock. He would send for her at nine o'clock. That was the time he had first interviewed her, and several times since she had had to report on his daughters' progress with their lessons at that hour.

Tension mounted within her with every passing second. With taut nerves she finally sprang to her feet and paced up and down restlessly. Suppose he turned her out this very night! Where would she go?

Somebody was coming! It was two minutes to nine! The summons was about to be delivered. Briefly she pressed her fingertips against her eyes as though to clear them in readiness to face more courageously whatever fate had in store for her. Then she lifted her strained white face and looked toward the door, letting her hands fall to her sides in an attitude of resignation. Motionless she waited and watched the handle turn.

The opening door revealed the last person she had expected to see. It was Robert who entered and closed the door after him. He met her startled, anxious eyes, but did not speak.

"Am I to go to your father's study now?" she asked in a tremulous voice.

The school table stood between them and he came across to lean on it with straight arms, his fingers curled over the edges, his gaze fixed steadily on her. "Set your mind at rest. Mother told me what happened. I managed to dissuade her from reporting the matter to my father."

She stared at him in incredulous relief, releasing her breath in a little gasp. Then abruptly she dropped her face into her hands, a flood of tears spilling from her eyes. Instantly he was beside her, taking her into his arms, holding her close. Her shoulders shook with her sobs. She was unable to control the paroxysm of relief, her head deeply bowed, her palms and fingers clamped like a mask over her features.

"Hush. Don't cry," he murmured, stroking her hair, but he did not mind how long she wept, delighting in the softness of her body pressed in complete unawareness against his, and he congratulated himself on having had the wit to seize the opportunity to put her into his debt when it had unexpectedly presented itself. "There's no need for tears. All is well. The incident is closed and forgotten."

His fingers moved to the back of her neck and he continued the sensual stroking under her hair until much of the desperate tautness went from her and she raised her head at last. She would have drawn back from him, but he pretended to be innocent of this move and did not relax his encircling arms.

"It was foolish of me to give way to tears," she gulped, drying her eyes on a cambric handkerchief, which she had taken with some difficulty from her skirt pocket, being hampered by his embrace, "but the relief was so great. I was expecting to be dismissed, and this last-minute reprieve overwhelmed me."

"I understand," he assured her softly. "I was glad to be able to intervene on your behalf."

"It was most kind of you, sir."

He shook his head impatiently at the formality of the manner in which she continued to address him. "Call me Robert!" he insisted quickly, intent on turning every aspect of the situation to his advantage. "That's my name. You know it well enough!"

She realized it was not much of a favor to ask of her in return for all he had done, but still she hesitated, the old caution rising in her, wary again of setting her feet on a sliding path that could bring her to the same end as that which had been so narrowly averted. "I don't think it would be wise for me—"

He interrupted her. "Please!" he urged fervently. "Where is the harm?"

She felt herself weaken, unable to resist the frantic appeal in his eyes. "Very well—Robert," she said with a shy, spontaneous smile.

A grin lit up his face. He tilted her chin with his fingers and his mouth closed down on hers with a speed and eagerness that took her completely by surprise. With a little moan of happiness she surrendered herself completely to the joy of kissing and being kissed, forgetful for a few ecstatic minutes of all the world and everything in it, conscious only of the man who held her in his arms, her own linked about his neck, having found their place there almost by their own volition.

His lips and hers hung lightly and moistly together in the last few seconds before disengagement, and he saw that she was more than a little dazed by the whirlpool of emotion that had made her a willing captive in his arms. He smiled down at her as she sank against his shoulder, and he gently brushed a tendril of her hair away from her cheek.

"Never have I felt like this before," he whispered lovingly, believing his own lie at such a moment of delight.

"Nor I," she breathed in perfect truthfulness.

"You are beautiful, Harriette." He meant those words with all his heart. She was beautiful with her hair slightly disarrayed and her lovely face aglow with a shy and transparent wonder at the depths of her feelings for him.

Blissfully she closed her eyes and opened them again as though she had never thought to hear such praise from the man she loved. "Dear Robert," she sighed almost inaudibly.

Keenly he pressed his new advantage home. "I hold you in such esteem, sweetheart. You cannot now deny me your company."

She was brought back to earth, having come the full circle by way of his kisses to circumstances that had been lifted from one danger only to be replaced by another. "Your parents would not approve," she protested unhappily, seeking to draw away from him, but he caught her hand in his and his arm around her became all the tighter.

"They need not know," he argued forcefully, "until the time comes when I choose to tell them."

He held her eyes, his meaning unmistakable. She understood that he meant to court her seriously, his intentions honorable, but still she tried to discourage him.

"It is out of the question. Your parents would never consent—"

His angry vehemence startled her. "What they say is of no importance! I'm of age and shortly to start a new career and a fresh life abroad! My future is in my own hands! I intend to plan it to suit myself and"—here his expression softened as his gaze roved over her face—"you too, Harriette."

He kissed her again, but gently this time and persuasively. Then he allowed her to release herself from his clinging embrace and move away from him. He saw that she was standing apart from him both mentally and physically in order to adjust to this new turn of events, her thoughts chaotic, and he feared that he might lose her yet.

"Meet me on Sunday afternoon," he pleaded. "You always go for a walk by yourself on the one free day you have in the week and should we be seen together there is no one who can say we did not meet accidentally."

Her back was toward him and he had no idea if his words had carried any weight, but he could tell she was gazing pensively before her. Wisely he said no more, knowing that she would make up her own mind and too much argument might prejudice his case, but he drew near to her, wanting her to be intensely aware of his presence, silently reminding her by the hairbreadth distance between them of the kisses they had shared and that she had only to turn to be in his arms again. Finally she answered him without looking round.

"I usually walk as far as the gardens of the park on Sunday afternoons. There is a bench under an oak tree, which gives me a pretty view of the lake."

He took her by the shoulders and turned her about to face him. "I'll be waiting for you there," he promised, taking her hand in both of his and curving her fingers as he put them to his lips. "Good night, sweet Harriette."

"Good night, Robert," she whispered in reply.

Left alone, she crossed her arm over her chest and placed the back of the fingers he had kissed against her face as though to transmit that magic touch of his lips. How could she wait for Sunday to come? Three whole days to be lived through before she could have him to herself again. Desperately she hoped that the weather would be fine, for summer was fading fast and soon the days would become autumnal, matching a certain chilliness that already touched the late hours through to early morning.

Undressing in her own room and wishing to let her thoughts dwell blissfully on all that Robert had said to her, she felt an angry resentment for the first time at the noisy bellowing of the strange Mr. Hardware somewhere in the neighboring house. She snatched up a shoe and ran across to hammer with the heel against the dividing wall.

"Be quiet in there, for mercy's sake!" she cried. But almost instantly all anger drained from her and she leaned back against the wall. What was the use? The man was not in the adjoining attic room and could not hear her, and even if he did it was doubtful that he would pay any attention, for it was surely true that his mind was unbalanced. She must not let him get on her nerves. Not now. Not when love had come to lighten any burden that she had to bear.

Sunday dawned bright and clear, dispelling any doubts she had had that the weather might mar the day. Her feet barely seemed to touch the ground when she set off in the afternoon, and she hurried along, not wanting to be late, but aware that it would be better not to be early either. Robert should be kept waiting about three or four minutes. Just enough to add spice to his eagerness to see her.

She timed her entrance into the park and did not hasten to their trysting place, but when the bench came into sight her heart sank. Robert was not there! Quickly she looked about her, hoping to see him coming toward her, but although there were many people strolling through the gardens there was no sign of him.

For a while she strolled about too, and then she sat and waited. An hour went by, and then another. It was time for her to return to Perbroke Square. She rose from the seat and, weighed down with disappointment, she looked neither to the right nor to the left, but made her way to the street and set off along it. When a carriage clattered to a halt within a few yards of her she was not aware of it until the door had been flung open and Mr. Sutcliffe sprang out to dash into her path.

"Good day, ma'am! We meet again!" He bowed his head, looking well pleased with himself, one arm outstretched as he tilted his cane at an angle.

She looked at him coldly. Their last encounter had resulted in her receiving a severe reprimand from Mr. Warrington, and a wave of animosity toward this stranger swept over her.

"You are not known to me, sir," she said, making a move to pass him by, but he sidestepped to block her way once again.

"Forgive me, I beg you. I should have presented myself through an intermediary, but that is not possible. Let our mutual acquaintance with the elusive Mr. Hardware suffice. I'm Benedict Sutcliffe—your servant, ma'am."

"I'm *not* acquainted with Mr. Hardware," she said crisply. "Good day to you, Mr. Sutcliffe." She gave him a curt nod of dismissal, but he was not to be easily brushed aside.

"I'm on my way to Perbroke Square. May I offer you a seat in my carriage, Miss—er?"

She would have refused without hesitation if at that moment her eye had not been caught by an open phaeton, which had gone bowling by in the direction along which she had come. In it sat Robert with a young woman at his side, and another man of about their age sat opposite them, all talking animatedly together. The hurt exploded inside her. Robert had not even remembered his promise to meet her, but had been dallying away the time in other company. Suddenly she could not bear that he might turn his head and see her.

She looked quickly back at Benedict Sutcliffe. "I am Miss Harriette Mead. I accept your kind offer of a ride to Perbroke Square—I am late already and have tarried far too long in the gardens."

"My delight and pleasure, Miss Mead."

He proffered a hand to assist her into the carriage, which she took, letting all her pent-up misery and humiliation direct itself toward him in an uncompromising animosity over which she had no control. Robert! Robert! Why is it not you instead of this dark stranger showing me consideration and attention? Did my kisses mean so little to you? Were your loving words completely false?

At any other time she would have appreciated the comfort of the carriage, which was richly upholstered in ruby velvet with gilt tassels dangling from the updrawn blinds at the windows, but now she paid it no attention. Benedict Sutcliffe seated himself in the opposite corner seat and rapped with his cane for the carriage to continue on its way. She kept her gaze fixed out the window as though she had never seen before the street that led to her present home, unable to be sure that her inner anguish would not be revealed upon her features, but she became uncomfortably aware of his dark-lashed scrutiny that did not waver. The silence between them seemed to become almost palpable, making her painfully aware of every breath he took, every slight swing of his crossed leg with the movement of the carriage, every tap of gloved finger against the shining surface of his cane.

"Do you go often to the park?" he inquired at last.

"No." To her dismay her voice had a choked note in it.

"Why not?"

"As a governess my hours of freedom are strictly limited," she said in calmer and more detached tones, having regained control of herself.

"I saw you that day with two little girls. Are they your only pupils?"

"Yes."

A silence fell again between them, but never once did that glittering stare leave her. She had the uncomfortable feeling that he guessed why she had accepted the ride, his alert eyes having missed nothing, and in some unaccountable way he was annoyed about it. Even jealous. But that was a ridiculous thought.

"I'm on my way, as you must have realized," he remarked, "to call on your neighbor again. I cannot believe he will go on refusing to see me if I call often enough."

"I would not put a wager on your chances," she said wryly. The carriage had turned into the Square.

His face relaxed into an amused half smile, his eyes almost disappearing between those black lashes. "I don't give up easily. People usually come to realize this in the end."

She was uncertain quite how to take this remark and concentrated on smoothing her gloves and looping the cord of her purse over her wrist in preparation to alight. "Thank you for bringing me home."

"I hope we shall meet again soon."

"Goodbye, Mr. Sutcliffe."

An hour later she was crossing the landing when Robert appeared at the door of his room, his face anxious and distressed. "I went out of town yesterday to visit friends in the country. There was a delay in my returning today. My horse went lame and some fellow guests at the house brought me back to London in their phaeton. Don't be angry with me, Harriette. I beg you!"

How could she be angry with him when the explanation was so simple and straightforward! Her whole face revealed her radiant forgiveness.

"There will be other Sunday afternoons," she said with a warm and tender smile, knowing that he wanted to embrace her in his relief, but neither of them dared make a single move toward the other, knowing that at any moment a door could open or someone come upon them unawares at any time.

"I cannot wait another week!" he insisted urgently, keeping his voice low. "Meet me in the garden this evening. At eleven o'clock. Everyone else will be safely abed."

There came a little burst of chatter from one of the upper landings as his sisters emerged from their room. Hastily she spoke in a whisper, passing him as she made for the stairs. "I will come at eleven—but only for a few minutes."

"Dearest!" he whispered back, going off in the opposite direction.

Looking up as she ascended the stairs, Harriette saw Nurse

Galloway turn away across the landing. Had the woman been spying on them? With a little frown Harriette continued on her way, consoling herself with the thought that no word that they had exchanged could have been overheard, although —on second thoughts—perhaps their softly spoken conversation had looked extraordinarily intimate when viewed from above, even though they had kept such a marked distance from each other. She must be careful. The nurse thrived on the jealous rivalry which existed traditionally between nursery and schoolroom, and although she herself wanted no part of it, there was no doubt that previous governesses had indulged in petty feuds with her.

The night was dark and starry when Harriette went out of the house by way of a door that led from the rear end of the long hall into a small vestibule, which was full of potted palms and fragrant flowers. Her feet were silent on the tiled floor, which threw off a gleam that helped show her the way, and she pressed down both handles of the narrow glass doors and opened them inward together, feeling the cool garden air sweep in on her.

Robert was waiting this time. He loomed up out of the darkness and swept her with him along the path and out of sight under the trees. There he drew her down beside him on a wrought-iron seat, snatching up both her hands and covering the palms with kisses. Then he lifted his head again and she saw the pale shape of his face in the darkness, his parted lips coming to claim hers. She swayed toward him from the waist, and his arms enfolded her with surprising gentleness, for he was tense and excited, breathing heavily, but she was unaware of the restraint he had put upon himself and surrendered her mouth to his soft kissing.

"We must see each other as often as possible," he whispered, resting his cheek on the top of her head as he held her close. "I must find a way for you to get in and out of the grounds unobserved after dark—"

"Robert! I dare not!" she cried fearfully, sitting upright in order to face him.

"Nonsense! There's nothing to be afraid of. I cannot take you to a play on Sunday afternoons, can I? And where can we dance by daylight? Wait until you see the lights of Vauxhall! You won't want the evening to end!"

"Is it as exciting a place as they say?" she asked yearningly.

"You shall see for yourself!"

"If only it were possible!"

"It can be arranged. Leave everything to me."

"Perhaps I could go to Vauxhall just once then!" she exclaimed impulsively, excitement at the thought running through her, "but I swear that I'll be almost dead with fright until I'm safely indoors again!"

He chuckled softly. "I'll make you forget Perbroke Square and the schoolroom and those wretched sisters of mine. You shall give them no thought when you're with me!"

His words served to remind her of her present danger. "I must go back indoors again," she insisted, glancing anxiously over her shoulder. "Suppose somebody came to check that the vestibule doors were locked and we were shut out here together!"

"I wouldn't mind," he whispered lovingly, nuzzling his face against hers.

She leaned away from him. "Perhaps not," she said, half smiling, half in reprimand, "but you would not be dismissed in disgrace in the morning. I cannot meet you here again, Robert. It is too risky."

"Then I shall meet you on your evening walk when you stroll around the Square for a little while before supper."

"You must not!" she protested frantically. "Your parents would see us and forbid it—or send me packing to be on the safe side!"

He laughed at her distress. "Extend your walk beyond the Square. There are narrow cobbled lanes that lead into a dozen small courtyards within a stone's throw of this house where we can linger for a few minutes of private conversation together. Is that too great a favor to grant me?"

She relented, partly through her desire to please him, and

also because she knew how much those few minutes alone with him every day would mean to her. "Very well. Until tomorrow evening, Robert."

He released her reluctantly, snatching one more kiss from her lips even as she turned to spring to her feet, which left joy glowing in her face as she fled back into the house.

It seemed to her that every stair creaked like a gunshot while she made for the safety of the attic floor, but each time she paused she could hear a rumble of activity in Mr. Hardware's house, which was different in some way from the usual hubbub and disturbance, and once she heard his front door slam.

Impelled by curiosity, wondering if Benedict Sutcliffe had managed to gain admittance somehow at this late hour of the night, she went into the schoolroom and crossed to the window. Looking down into the darkened Square she saw two carriage lamps shining like yellow eyes in front of Mr. Hardware's house, but she realized at once that it was not Benedict's elegant equipage, for it was longer and narrower with only two horses between the shafts. A man in a cloak, probably the driver, paced slowly up and down, smoking a pipe as he waited. Had Mr. Hardware actually received some visitors at last? Or was he moving house in the night as Mrs. Warrington hoped he would do?

Then she gave a gasp, pressing closer to the window. The front door of Number Eighteen had opened, throwing a rectangle of light down the steps and across the pavement to the vehicle, which she saw now was a hearse! Even as she watched, black shadows were cast within the patch of light as two men, bearing a coffin between them, emerged from the cover of the portico. Almost at once the front door was shut after them, wiping the gruesome little scene from her sight, but not before she had seen that the coffin was too small to have contained the mortal remains of Mr. Hardware. It was his housekeeper who was being moved to her last resting place in the dark hours of the night!

Harriette drew back quickly against the wall, averting her

face, touched by a chill of horror and unnerved by what she had seen. Mr. Hardware was left alone in the house next door. Would he continue to rant and rave with no one under his own roof to hear him, or would it prove to be as she suspected and his blunderings and shoutings were concerned with a private agony of mind that had nothing to do with anyone else?

This question was answered for her in the early hours of the morning when the now familiar but still inexplicable crash resounded against the wall and dashed sleep from her. She lay in her bed listening to the muffled bellowings of his voice and the thumping of his footsteps. It was like hearing the bewildered roarings of a great animal held captive within a cage of its own making, having no idea how to get out.

In spite of her conviction that nothing could break down the intervening wall, she was more afraid than she had ever been before. She lighted a candle and sat up in bed, her shawl wrapped around her shoulders, and did not blow the flame out again until peace returned to the house next door with the first pale glimmer of dawn.

# *Four*

As THE LAST DAYS OF SUMMER turned to deep autumn, Harriette lived only to be with Robert. She came to know every corner and gate and door of the cobbled lanes where they strolled each evening when it was fine, and when it rained they took refreshment in a small coffeehouse, but always their time together was brief, for she dared not be too long away.

Only when he took her to Vauxhall and Old Drury did they have longer together, but the necessity of slipping back into the house unseen at a late hour presented such difficulties that the pleasure of the outings was spoiled.

It was a bitter blow to her when their evening walks together were brought abruptly to an end. Mr. Warrington happened to see her leaving the house and called her back, saying that she must be content with the daily exercise she took with the girls and not venture out in the evenings again until it was spring once more and the days were longer.

Harriette hoped that when spring came again she would be in India with Robert, but in the meantime the happiest hours of her everyday existence had been taken from her. In disappointment she turned and went back to the attic, knowing that Robert must wait in vain for her coming.

At the schoolroom window, her forehead and palms resting against the glass, she peered out across the poorly lit Square. Robert would be on the corner now, looking up and down, impatiently consulting his watch, and wondering why she had not appeared.

He would soon become irritable, she knew. He had a habit of sulking when things did not always go his way, a family failing that she saw often enough in both Phoebe and his mother. She gave a long, slow sigh.

At bedtime she stood in her long white nightgown, brushing her hair before the small swing glass, which occupied the center of the chest of drawers, her thoughts full of Robert. How long had he waited before giving up hope that she would come? Having become so used to the protest of floorboards and timbers at the disturbances caused by Mr. Hardware, she paid no attention to the faint creak of her own door and did not realize that it was opening. Not until Robert was in the room with the door closed again behind him was she aware that he was there, his reflection smiling at her in the swing glass.

She lowered the brush and spun round in wide-eyed dismay. "Robert! What on earth are you doing here?"

"I had to see you." His tone was slightly truculent, very much as she had expected, but she failed to see that it was more in disappointment at a lack of welcome, which he had optimistically anticipated, than rooted in an earlier disappointment at her failing to turn up at their meeting place.

"That's no reason to come up to the attics!" She snatched up her shawl from the back of the chair and swept it about her with a flurry of tasseled fringe.

He advanced a few steps toward her. "I had to find out why you didn't meet me."

"Your father has forbidden me to go out walking after dark! I can't see you any more in the evenings!"

He thumped an angry fist against the bedpost, frowning wrathfully at the news. "Damn him! He's forever interfering in my affairs."

"He didn't know that I went out to meet you!"

Robert gave a sour laugh. "That makes no difference. He manages to spoil everything for me whether he is aware of the reason or not. I shall be thankful when the time comes to be free of him." He held out his arms to her. "Then we'll be able to do exactly as we like."

She backed away from him, the shawl clutched high under her chin. "But you are not free yet, and neither am I! We're still under his roof! In London! You must leave my room at once! I refused to let you come to the schoolroom because it was too dangerous! But this is sheer madness!"

"Why?" he coaxed, smiling. "Have we not a right to be together?"

"Not in my room!"

"There is nothing to worry about. My parents went out to dine in company and won't be back yet."

"That is not the point!"

"I disagree." He raised his arms invitingly once more. "Come to me, my dearest."

She shook her head violently, making her hair swirl about her face. "Merciful God! If you should be discovered in this part of the house—!" She bit her trembling lip.

"Who could do that?" he teased, determined to brush away her fears.

"The servants! You may have been seen!"

He compressed his lips, losing his smile. "Nobody saw me. Do you think I'm a fool? The coast was clear."

"You can't be sure!"

He lost patience altogether. "Perhaps I wish I could be found here! It would be all for the better! Our being discovered together in a somewhat compromising situation—to put it mildly!—would ensure the sweeping away of any opposition to our marriage."

Her eyes narrowed incredulously. "How can you talk such nonsense! I'd be told to pack my belongings together and I'd find myself out in the street five minutes after that! In the dead of night! With nowhere to go!"

"I'd come with you!" He drew closer to her, tired already of the argument.

"Then we should both be destitute! You've grumbled often enough about your debts and the meager amount left for spending from your allowance. Even that small sum would be withdrawn by Mr. Warrington, and then how should we live until it was time for you to sail to India?"

"I have friends. They would help." He had little real interest in what he was saying, touching her hair and curling a shining tendril of it about his finger, desire for her running hot and thick in his veins. "I'd raise a loan and pay them back later."

"No! No! No!" She continued to move backward, he moving with her, until her shoulder blades became pressed against the cold plaster of the wall dividing her attic room from the one next door. "Your father wanted you to start your new career with all debts cleared, and I agree with him. Too many men get caught in the mire of early gambling indiscretions, which drag at them while they are forever incurring new obligations in a vain effort to cut free. I have told you that I will not go to India on a ticket purchased with borrowed money, creating fresh debts to encumber you."

"I want us to travel together."

"We've known from the start that would not be possible. You must send for me independently, and in the meantime I must remain in employment. I have no choice!"

He set the flat of his hands on the wall either side of her and lowered his head to bring his mouth within an inch of hers. "How can you be so infernally practical in the face of love?" he questioned wryly, not wholly in jest.

"I've had to be practical for as long as I can remember!" She knew she must be stern with him, the pattern set already for his dependence on her as the stronger character. "I cannot change now."

But he had ideas of his own to soften and sway her out of her present stubborn mood, intending to bring her through the vulnerability of her heightened senses to a degree of intimacy that would not have been possible in the normal run of circumstances. He had played the pining suitor too long to her natural modesty. With throbbing excitement he saw how she started, her eyes widening at him, when he closed in on her. With a groan of appeal, holding her captive between his body and the wall, his caressing hands slid the soft cotton of her nightgown over her smooth contours. She gasped some protest, but he was beyond listening, intent on discovery, and when he found that she was averting her lips he grabbed her chin and clamped his mouth down on hers, smothering all sound from her.

The sheer discomfort of having her head jammed against the wall defeated his attempts to caress her into submission, and open-eyed she struggled violently within his grasp and wrenched her mouth from his.

"Please go, Robert," she implored in a choked whisper, the rigidity of her body a complete rejection. Whether he would have obeyed her she was never to know, for in the same instant a great shout went up within the next-door house, and when it was followed by a tremendous crashing and banging that echoed and re-echoed he loosened his vise-like grip on her in a kind of guilt-ridden alarm. It was a terrifying fracas, louder than anything she had ever heard before, and even to her mind there leaped thoughts of murder being done.

"What in hell's name is that?" he exclaimed in bewilderment.

Before she could answer there rose a shrill screaming from the floor below. She knew it to be from Caroline and guessed she had been awakened with a start of terror by the thundering noise and her vivid imagination.

"That's your sister!" she gasped. "I must go to her!"

He caught her by the shoulder and jerked her back. "There's no need for you to appear on the scene! That old devil in the next house made enough noise to wake the dead, and Caroline, the foolish child, has taken fright."

"It's more than that! She believes it is a dragon that she hears blundering about next door! I must reassure her!"

"Her nurse will be there!"

"The woman is stupid and does not understand!" She tore herself free and flew from him out of the room and down the stairs.

She found the nurse beating Caroline with the flat of her hard hand in an effort to stem the shrieking, shuddering sobs. Harriette thrust her off and sat down on the bed, gathering the frenzied child onto her lap. "You're safe, Caroline," she said soothingly, trapping the flailing limbs within her embrace and rocking her gently to and fro. "There's no dragon next door. It was only old Mr. Hardware throwing a few pots and pans about the place. The din made you wake in a fright. That was all."

The nurse thrust her ugly face wrathfully toward Harriette. "This is my domain, Miss Mead! You have no right—no right at all!—to come interfering in this manner! Go back to your attic where you belong!"

Harriette took no notice. She went on quietening the sobbing, shaking child, her calm tones having effect, and she paid no attention to the nurse's tirade and her threats that Mr. and Mrs. Warrington should be told about it when they returned from the soirée they were attending. Phoebe, who had come from her own room to watch with malicious enjoyment the spectacle of Caroline making a stupid fuss, received the full force of the nurse's wrath and with a stinging wallop she was chased howling back to bed.

"Listen to me," Harriette said to Caroline as soon as they were alone, drying the child's eyes with a corner of the sheet. "You must try to understand that poor Mr. Hardware is lonely in that big house on his own. He has nobody to talk to. That is why he shouts about and sounds exactly like a roaring dragon. Is there any way I can prove to you that it is he whom you have heard—and nothing else?"

Caroline gulped. "I'd believe you if you'd been in there and seen for yourself. Otherwise I cannot and I am so frightened." Her eyes brimmed over with tears again and she buried her face against Harriette's neck, clinging tightly to her.

Harriette pondered the problem while she continued to comfort the child. Only one possible solution presented itself to her, and it was hard not to shudder away the thought of it. She could enter Mr. Hardware's garden one dark evening and peer in the downstairs windows at the back of the house where Caroline thought the dragon was kept. Then she could truthfully tell the child that she had looked in and seen nothing. She was certain she would be called to task if the venture reached Mrs. Warrington's ears, but surely settling Caroline's fears once and for all would outweigh the means taken to do it.

She looked down and saw that Caroline had fallen asleep, the tears still wet on her lashes. Carefully she laid her back on the pillows and tucked her up again. Coming out of the room, she happened to glance down the stairs to the floor below and saw that the nurse had seated herself on a chair, ready to waylay Mr. and Mrs. Warrington with a full report of all that had happened when they returned from the soirée. Well, Harriette thought, treading on the nurse's toes was not a very serious matter, and the very worst that could be expected was a reprimand from Mrs. Warrington in the morning. At the moment she felt too weary to worry about that.

To her relief Robert had gone from her room. She blew out the candle and climbed into bed. That night she dreamed of raindrops tapping with a persistence that did not ease, but when she awoke in the morning there was no sign of rain and the fog was thick against the window.

During the day, Harriette thought again about Caroline's increasing terror and could see no alternative to her plan. She also confessed to herself her own growing curiosity to see into the next-door house and to learn something of the reasons for the terrible sounds. She decided she would have to choose her moment and climb over the garden wall. It should be easy enough, although it was about eight feet high. A stone terrace conveniently shortened the height on the Warringtons' side, and a light ladder borrowed from the stable could be lowered down on the other side.

It took two days before she could get the ladder and conceal it in the bushes. The fog helped her, and on the third evening after supper had been served to her and cleared away she got a lamp out of the cupboard and put it ready. Then she changed into her oldest dress, not wanting to soil her better ones, and set off down the stairs. She saw no need for stealth. She was at liberty to take the air in the garden even though the fog was thick as porridge. It was no concern of the servants, and the family were in their own apartments. Whether Robert was in or out she did not know, but if she met him she would tell him what she was about and hope that he would come with her.

But she reached the glass doors that led out into the garden without seeing anybody. Out into the fog she went, her lamp giving a tiny glow of light against the gray blanket that enfolded her on all sides. She found the ladder where she had left it, and carried it with her up the steps of the terrace. A stone seat gave her a firm base on which to stand while lifting the ladder over to the other side. When it was firmly in position she stepped onto the back of the seat and settled herself on the top of the wall.

Her heart was beating wildly when she began the descent into the wilderness next door. Twigs and branches caught at her clothes and the whole place smelled wet and sour and neglected. The tall grass rustled about her as she moved cautiously toward the house. The black, unlit eyes of the downstairs windows loomed up at her. She opened the lamp, which she had closed in fear of its glow being seen, and pressed it against the glass. The light showed her a drawing room similar to the corresponding one in the Warringtons' house, but it was completely bare. Not a stick of furniture to be seen. The other ground-floor room was the same.

Then she noticed that one of the glass doors to a rear vestibule stood slightly open. Perhaps she had better look inside in order to be able to tell Caroline that not even the vestibule contained a dragon. She held her lamp high and put her head in through the gap, her heart palpitating painfully, and she saw that the door into the house from the vestibule also stood open, and then her lamplight was lost in the pitch blackness that swallowed up the feeble outskirts of the glow.

Suddenly she felt a tug on her skirt hem. Her heart seemed to stop, so powerful was the wave of horror that swept over her. Slowly she looked down, not knowing what she would see. Her eyes widened, her pupils dilating, and she screamed out on an ear-splitting note that sent an owl flying up with an eerie flutter of wings from a tree. A man's hand, big and gnarled, had stretched out through the open crack of the door and was lying with blood-stained palm uppermost, the fingers holding on to her.

She whipped her skirt free and rushed panic-stricken from that terrible place. In her terror she blundered blindly through the trees and the undergrowth, forgetting where she had left the ladder, sobbing with fright, the fog confusing her. She finally found it by feeling her way along the wall, scratching her hands in the process, stumbling over stones and broken pots. With a gasp of relief she scrambled back over the wall, and as she jumped down from the seat a low howl reached her through the fog.

Clapping her hands over her ears, she ran back along the terrace and into the house. She had one thought in her head and that was to find Robert. She threw open the library door, but he was not there. Along she raced to his room and hammered on the door, but there was no reply. With a rasping sob she turned away and leaned against the wall, covering her face with her hands. The cold horror of that moment when she had looked down and seen that hand engulfed her anew.

"Harriette? What are you doing here?" Robert's voice asked in surprise. He had come up from the drawing room.

She rolled her head around, but could not answer him. Her teeth were chattering with shock and her cheeks were hollow. He took her by the shoulders and his tone became anxious.

"What's happened?" he demanded.

She tilted forward in a faint and would have fallen if he had not scooped her up in his arms.

When she recovered consciousness she was lying on her own bed and Robert was sitting beside her, rubbing her wrists, and a cold, wet cloth had been laid on her forehead.

"Whatever upset you and made you faint?" he questioned urgently when he saw her open her eyes, making no inquiry as to how she was feeling. "Have my parents discovered that we've been meeting?"

She took the cloth away from her head. "Nothing like that," she answered weakly. "How cold I am." She made an effort to sit up and he put his arm about her to hold her close, supporting her against his body as he sat on the bed beside her, and he pulled up the covers to wrap them about her.

"What was it then?" he asked with evident relief that the reason was not what he had feared.

She told him all that happened. He listened intently, and when she described seeing the hand in a shuddering whisper she saw an incredulous glint show in his eye.

"You don't believe me," she said dully.

He bent his head and kissed her cheek. "I believe you saw *something*," he said, measuring his words, "but I'm more inclined to think that in the fog and the darkness you mistook a fallen rake or some other garden implement for a hand."

"I tell you I saw it," she insisted stubbornly. "It was— horrible."

He gathered her closer to him and smiled down into her upturned face. "You are as impressionable as Caroline. Your imagination played you tricks. In the morning light you will realize that I'm right. Don't think about it any more, my dearest. Look at me. Look into my eyes. I will make you forget everything except the fact that we love each other and are alone together."

She did love him. She dreaded the time when he would leave for India and the long months of waiting that must pass before he could send for her. Her arms closed about his neck and she gave herself up to the joy of his ardent kisses, not wanting him to leave her alone in that hated room, but knowing that she could not let him stay more than a few more minutes when each second held the ever-present risk of discovery. Neither of them heard the door open.

"Robert! What is the meaning of this?"

They broke apart. Mr. Warrington stood in the doorway, his face crimson with rage, his jowls quivering. Behind him

Nurse Galloway peered vindictively over his shoulder, not wanting to miss anything of the scene being played out before her, and Harriette was left in no doubt as to who had reported seeing Robert carrying her up to her room. Slowly she swung her feet to the floor and stood up. Fate had stepped in and Robert would have to declare his intentions toward her far sooner than they had intended after all. So be it. She looked toward Robert. He had turned ashen and he faced his father defiantly.

"Send that damn nurse away!" he demanded. "I'll not have her listening to every word we say!"

"In a minute!" Mr. Warrington snapped. "I say, in a minute! Nurse has a statement to make. A statement that I want you both to hear. Both of you, I say."

The woman sidled forward, and her shifty glance leapt from Harriette to Robert and back again, although she addressed her master. "This isn't the first time Mr. Robert has been to Miss Mead's room, sir. He was here on the night of the soirée, only I daren't mention the matter to you in the hearing of the mistress. I saw him come down from her room with my own eyes when Miss Mead had left him to stop Miss Caroline from screaming over a nightmare. Then there was another occasion when he was a long time alone with her in the schoolroom. I went up there to get a book that Miss Phoebe wanted and I saw Miss Mead in Mr. Robert's arms. Fine goings on, I must say!" She gave an emphatic nod of her capped head, making its frill ripple. "And then Miss Mead dares to interfere and tell me how to treat my own charges when her immoral behavior should bar her from teaching innocent children—"

"That is enough!" Mr. Warrington ordered, silencing her. He looked directly at his son. "Do you deny these accusations?"

Robert's gaze did not waver. He had recovered himself. "A pack of lies, sir!" he said in a hard voice. "Send the wretch away and I'll give you the true version!"

The nurse departed, her mouth opening and shutting in

outraged indignation. Harriette clasped her hands nervously. Who would have thought that they had been spied upon in such a savage way?

Mr. Warrington set his feet more squarely apart, and linked his hands under his coattails. "Truth or lies, the nurse shall leave in the morning. I will have no tattle tongues in my household to start gossip and scandal circulating beyond these walls. Well? I am waiting! I tell you I am waiting."

Robert gave a shrug. "I did come to the schoolroom once, but it was with a message for Miss Mead from Mama, which she will verify. But apart from that one occasion I have not been up here until tonight," he continued glibly, ignoring the startled look that Harriette gave him, "and I should not have come on this occasion if Miss Mead hadn't involved herself in some ridiculous escapade that took her climbing over the wall to play some prank, shining lights into old Mr. Hardware's windows."

"Robert!" Harriette breathed, aghast.

Mr. Warrington swung around toward her. "Is that the reason for your disheveled state? The mud on your gown?"

"Yes," Harriette faltered, "but—"

"Enough! That is enough! Carry on, Robert."

Robert deliberately avoided Harriette's eyes. "Miss Mead became frightened in the fog and imagined she saw hands clawing at her. She appeared to faint and I carried her up here to her bed." He took a deep breath. "When she put her arms about me I admit that I found it impossible to resist her."

Mr. Warrington's beady eyes under their pouched lids regarded his son thoughtfully. "Hmm. I accept your explanation. I accept it. It is timely that your departure to India has been brought forward. Most timely. You can forget all about this unfortunate affair. Your mother was afraid that you might—well, no matter. Be off with you and put her mind at rest."

Dumbly Harriette watched Robert hurry from the room. He did not give her a backward glance, anxious to make his escape. He had not told her that his plans had been altered, choosing to keep his almost imminent departure from her, no thought in his head of ever sending for her. He had lied to her. Lied all the way. Now he had abandoned her, relegating all responsibility, not caring what happened to her. Not caring at all. She became vaguely aware that Mr. Warrington was speaking to her.

"You stand silent, Miss Mead. Silent. It is wise of you. Now I am a humane man, as I told you when you came to my house. Humane. Therefore you may remain under my roof until the morning. Be out of my house by six o'clock. Do you understand? Eh? Six o'clock and not a second later." He cleared his throat. "I will also remind you that you have failed far short of the three-month trial period. Far short. Do not expect a penny piece from me. Not a penny piece, I say. I bid you good night and goodbye, Miss Mead." The door closed after him.

She put her hand on the end of the bed and hung on to it for support. The hurt that had seared through her at Robert's betrayal had mercifully numbed her for the time being. She could feel nothing. Neither fear of the precarious future facing her nor grief for the love she had lost. The time would come for tears, but it was not now. Her face felt stiff and her whole body was shaking from the effect of one shock on top of another, her flesh like ice. She must put on some warmer clothes or she might develop some fever and then what would become of her if she were ill? With unsteady movements she went to the cupboard and took out what she needed. There was no thought in her head of sleep. She must pack her belongings and have everything ready. Slowly she moved about the room, taking down her pictures and folding up the cloth she had embroidered for the top of the chest of drawers.

When all she owned was packed away she took the candle and went back into the schoolroom. Gaps showed on the shelves where she had removed her own books, and the weaving loom, which had interested both Phoebe and Caroline, was now at the bottom of her trunk. She sat down at the table and took out a sheet of paper to write to Caroline.

She knew that she would not see her in the morning, and she wanted to tell her that she had seen for herself that there were no dragons in Mr. Hardware's house. That much good at least could come out of the whole terrible incident.

When the letter was finished she shook sand on it before folding it up and sealing it. Then she left it on the mantel shelf where it would be seen.

There were a lot of papers to be thrown away and she crushed them into the fireplace and added some sticks and a few pieces of coal to make a little fire. Drawing up the chair to the warmth, she sank down onto it to wait for morning to come. It was very still both in the house and next door. She dozed, dreamed, and woke with a start, her heart hammering.

She looked about her uneasily, and moved her chair nearer to the rosy embers of the fire. It was uncannily silent. Mr. Hardware had not made a single disturbance since three nights ago, when it had sounded as if the whole interior of the house had gone crashing about his ears. That was strange. During all the weeks she had been with the Warringtons he had clattered about at some time during every night, but now even tonight was passing without a whisper. There had been the tapping the same night of the crash, of course. But she had dreamed that, hadn't she? Or had she lain between sleep and consciousness, thinking it was rain against the window? Instead, could it have been his stick against the wall somewhere, feebly trying to attract attention?

She sat up very straight in the chair. Suppose—suppose that tremendous noise had been caused by his falling down somewhere. He was alone in the house. Nobody would have gone to his aid. And suppose, finding that tapping aroused no alarm and brought no help, he had managed to drag himself into the vestibule, but his shouts for help had gone unheard. And when she had come by chance to that half-open door he had reached out and clutched at her skirt in desperation and she had turned away from him, as Robert had from her.

She sprang to her feet, glad to have something to do. It had been Mr. Hardware's hand that she had seen! Why had he

71

not spoken to her? She remembered the grisly howl that had followed her and her blood chilled at the memory of it.

Hurrying into the bedroom, she went to the window and looked out. The fog still masked everything in the early-morning darkness. Was Mr. Hardware still lying helpless in the vestibule, hurt and perhaps dying? She must help him. The ladder was where she had left it. The lantern she had lost somewhere in her flight, but there was another in the schoolroom cupboard. She had to go back. And there was no time to waste.

She was almost thankful for the numbed state of her emotions. It helped to keep fear at bay when she crept out of the house once more and hurried along the terrace to climb the stone seat again. The possibility did cross her mind that the commotion three nights ago could have been caused by foul play and heaven alone knew what she might find in the vestibule, but she could not turn back. She had to discover if help *was* needed.

She stepped off the ladder and pushed her way through the tangled undergrowth again to reach the bleak, unlit house.

"Mr. Hardware?" she called softly. "Are you there?"

Her lantern showed her the half-open door, but there was no sign of the hand that she had seen before, and just for a few seconds she wondered if Robert had been right and her imagination had played her tricks in the fog.

She pushed the door gently. It opened a few more inches and then jammed against something. Warily she entered and shone her lantern down on the floor. The huge old man lay sprawled on his side, one arm covering his face, his thick white hair tied back into an outmoded queue with a scrap of frayed ribbon. His coat was of coarse brown cloth, the brass buttons shining in the lantern light, and his breeches were blue, although one knee was strapped into the cup of a wooden peg leg, the base of which was splintered and broken.

She dropped down onto her knees at his side. "I've come back to help you, Mr. Hardware! Please speak to me! Don't let me be too late!"

He made no sound. Trying to prepare herself for some pox-ruined visage, she carefully drew his arm away from his face and it flopped heavily to the floor, the gold ring on his finger hitting the tiles with a clink. He was a dreadful color, purplish veins staining the unnatural pallor of his complexion, but apart from having lost the right eye and bearing a great scar across one cheekbone, his leonine features were not unsightly, and in his youth he must have been a man of masterly appearance. She put her fingertips against his neck. He was alive! She could feel the faint, irregular pulse.

Then she started violently. The pouched lid of his good eye lifted and a fearsome blue eye glinted at her, oddly alive in a face dragged down on the right side by an apoplectic seizure that must have taken the power of speech from him. She recognized the symptoms, having seen her own father thus afflicted.

She took his cold, immobile hand into both of hers and held it tightly and reassuringly. "I've come to help you, Mr. Hardware," she said slowly and precisely, wanting him to understand, "but first of all I must fetch the doctor."

The blue eye closed under the frown of the thicket of eyebrow above it and almost imperceptibly he gave a shake of his head. She understood what it must mean to him as a recluse to have his home invaded by strangers, but he needed a doctor, and as quickly as possible.

"I'll fetch Dr. Fielder, who lives across the Square," she told him. "You must have seen him often enough from your window. He will have you moved to your bed and arrange for you to be looked after."

To her dismay a tear rolled out from under the closed lid and a despairing gurgle uttered from his throat. "I must do what is best for you," she said, her voice choked by compassion. His hand stirred slightly and he held on to hers in a feeble grip, but she comprehended what he was trying to ask her. "Never fear! I will come back to you. I swear it!"

With the aid of the lantern she made her way into the house. Seeing some cloaks on a row of pegs, she scooped them all down and quickly covered Mr. Hardware with them before continuing on her way again and reaching the hall. The door was chained and bolted from top to bottom, and she saw how impossible it would have been for Mr. Hardware to unbolt it. Then she was racing down the portico steps and across the Square.

The doctor's servants were up and about. There was the glimmer of candlelight in the ground-floor rooms. She jerked the bellpull and then banged the knocker hard. A footman in a fustian jacket opened the door. She did not give him a chance to ask what she wanted at such an early hour.

"I must speak to Dr. Fielder! It's urgent. Mr. Hardware at Number Eighteen will die if the doctor does not attend him at once!"

The footman did not tell her to call back later as she had feared, but asked her name and bade her come in and wait. A few minutes later the butler came and questioned her, and then he in turn fetched the valet, who agreed, after some frantic persuasion on her part, to rouse his master.

Dr. Fielder, once summoned, did not delay long before he appeared fully dressed, a leather bag in his hand. He was a short, stocky man with silver-brown hair, his face stern, but not unkindly. Quickly she explained the situation, and he summoned two footmen to accompany him.

She led the way back across the Square at a run. In the vestibule she threw herself down on her knees beside the prostrate figure.

"I'm back," she said breathlessly. Mr. Hardware did not react in any way, his eye remained closed, and he was barely breathing. Fear clutched at her. Was it too late after all?

Anxiously she watched Dr. Fielder stoop down to give the patient a quick examination. Then he straightened up and told the footmen to make a stretcher of a rug or anything else they could find to carry the patient up to bed.

"It's a clear case of an apoplexy, Miss Mead," the doctor said. "No doubt it brought about the fall, which caused him to break his good leg in two places. He must be exceptionally strong not to have expired instantly, and how he has managed to keep alive since is beyond my understanding. I'll have to bleed him before I can attempt to set the limb. Shall you assist me, Miss Mead? Or have you no stomach for such a task?"

"I'll help in any way I can," she answered swiftly.

While the patient was being lifted onto his own cloak, swift search on the ground floor having shown only rooms barren of furnishings, Harriette hurried upstairs to find Mr. Hardware's bedroom. The next two floors were equally bare, although a solitary chair was placed close to the window in the room facing the Square on the second floor, from which he had viewed all who had passed by.

The third floor proved to be his living quarters, the furniture old, but well made, and his four-poster bed had velvet hangings, which had once been quite sumptuous but were now faded and worn, the gilt tassels black and tarnished. The linen on it left much to be desired, having been left unchanged for a long time, but a quick hunt in the cupboards resulted in her discovering folded blankets and a stack of sheets and pillowcases, somewhat yellowed by long storage. Quickly she ripped everything from the bed and made it up afresh. She was laying out a clean nightshirt when the two footmen, followed by Dr. Fielder, carried their burden into the room. Before leaving again the footmen undressed the sick man and put him into the nightshirt. Harriette collected together clean towels, a bowl, and other things that the doctor would need. When they were alone Dr. Fielder set to work, and she helped him calmly and competently, anticipating his instructions. He questioned her as to how she came to be the one who had discovered Mr. Hardware when no one of his acquaintance in the Square had ever clapped eyes on the man, and she spoke up frankly and told him why she had gone alone there and what had happened.

When the bloodletting was over and the patient's broken leg had been set in splints, Harriette drew the covers over him and smoothed the sheet under his chin, reminded of the countless times she had done the very same thing for her father.

"I can tell you have had considerable nursing experience, Miss Mead," Dr. Fielder said, rolling down his sleeves.

"Yes, I have, Doctor."

"Then you'll know how to feed the patient. A few spoonfuls of clear broth later, if he is able to take it. A sip of egg wine. Unless a fever develops I see no reason why a man of such phenomenal strength as Mr. Hardware—in spite of his age—should not recover."

She looked at him across the bed. "You are leaving me in charge?"

"Why not?" he answered briskly, putting on his coat. "You told me yourself that you have been dismissed from Mr. and Mrs. Warrington's employ and have yet to apply for another post. This should suit you admirably until such time as Mr. Hardware is able to make his own arrangements." His eyes narrowed astutely and he paused in straightening his collar. "Unless you are nervous of being left alone with a sick and helpless man in this rather unusual house without servants or other company?"

She considered the question. There was a lot about Mr. Hardware and the house that she did not understand, but her feeling of compassion for him momentarily outweighed all else. "I'm not afraid," she said quietly. "At least, not so afraid as I was when the interior of this house was a mystery to me and I knew nothing about it. It is still a mystery, of course, but now I stand at the center of it and that puts me in command."

"Well spoken. You're a sensible young woman." He picked up his bag. "I will call in again later today."

She accompanied him down to the door, and when he had set off across the Square she went up the steps to Number Seventeen and rang the bell. It was full daylight and long after the hour when she had been told to depart from the Warringtons' household. The footman who answered the door merely assumed that she had been out looking for work and had returned for her belongings, but his face became a mask of blank astonishment when she asked him if he would be kind enough to carry her trunk into the house next door. He obliged willingly, eager to catch a glimpse inside the house that aroused such curiosity among those belowstairs, but, as he told the other servants afterward, he saw only the unfurnished hall and had neither sight nor sound of the owner himself.

# *Five*

HARRIETTE HAD BEEN NURSING MR. HARDWARE for almost
three weeks when she happened to catch sight of Robert's
departure for India. She had been thankful for the opportunity
to work hard, suppressing her own troubles in the fight to
keep alive the old man who lay unstirring in the great bed,
barely conscious. She had explored the house, but had avoided
the attic, not wanting to pry, knowing that it had been a kind
of retreat for him. She had discovered that although he resided entirely on the third floor, uncannily like a besieged
nobleman seeking the safest part of a surrounded castle, he
appeared to have taken meals in the basement kitchen, where
she had found the cupboard surprisingly well stocked. Getting daily supplies presented no problems, it having been Mr.
Hardware's custom to leave notes for the tradesmen, who
delivered everything from meat and fish and pies to milk,
firewood, sausages, and fowls.

Dr. Fielder, perhaps anxious that there should be no delay
in the paying of his bill, contacted Mr. Hardware's lawyer,
Mr. Bellamy-Jones, who called promptly after being notified
of his client's illness. Having satisfied himself from Harriette's
testimonials that she was completely trustworthy, although
it was deucedly odd finding a young woman of intelligence
prepared to perform the most menial tasks for an old, sick
hulk of a man, he proceeded to arrange her wages, and gave
her extra money to pay the tradesmen, instructing her to keep
accurate accounts in order that he might peruse them when-

ever he called. But he would tell her nothing about Mr. Hardware, no details of how he had spent his life, or whether he had ever been married. All she learned was that the housekeeper, who had been with Mr. Hardware for about twenty years, had died peacefully in her sleep, and Mr. Bellamy-Jones had been called to arrange the funeral, but afterward Mr. Hardware had refused to employ anyone to take her place.

"He will send you packing as soon as he recovers his faculties," Mr. Bellamy-Jones had warned. "Has he spoken yet?"

"Not a word."

"Do you know whereabouts he fell?"

"On the flight of stairs leading down to the hall. The balustrade is broken, and I found gouge marks and splintered wood."

It was a wonder that Mr. Hardware had not killed himself outright. Several times while watching over him she had been afraid that the struggle to survive would prove too much for him. Her nursing had been tireless, and although not once had he opened that fierce, almost evil eye, he obeyed whenever she coaxed him to take some of the invalid food which she prepared with such care and spooned into his mouth with endless patience.

There had been comfort in looking after him, knowing that she was needed, but suddenly the final blow of Robert leaving without a word left her floundering in an abyss of despair.

She had strolled across the empty drawing room while her patient was sleeping, to look idly out at the Square. And there was Robert, dressed in new traveling clothes, saying farewell to his parents and sisters on the steps of the portico. The coach, which was waiting to carry him away, was loaded with his trunks and boxes, ready for shipment.

Perhaps he sensed her anguished gaze, because at the moment of turning to step into the coach he happened to glance up over his shoulder and saw her holding the curtain back to look down at him. Hostility and shame flared in his eyes. Then he looked away again, threw himself into the equipage, and slammed the door. He leaned out to wave once to the family group he was leaving behind, but withdrew by the time the coach had covered a few yards, although Phoebe and Caroline ran a little way along the pavement to wave after him with their handkerchiefs until he was quite out of sight.

Blindly she stumbled back to the sickroom and sank down on the chair at the bedside where she had spent many watching hours. Drooping forward, she leaned her arms on the bed, her face in the crook of them, and let her sobbing rack her.

"Oh, Robert! Robert!" she cried over and over again. "I loved you! I loved you!"

In her unhappiness she did not notice the touch on her arm, but when it was repeated she lifted her head with a start and turned her tear-stained face toward the patient. He had raised his hand from the coverlet to rest his fingers against her arm. His wrinkled old eye was fixed on her, not balefully, but with a kind of wry sympathy.

"Don' weep," he said slowly in a slurred, uncultured voice. "Neve' did like to see a prett' woman weep." His eye closed and his hand slipped back into its indentation on the coverlet.

"You spoke to me!" she exclaimed, sobs still choking her. "You're going to get well again."

He shook his head almost imperceptibly. "Too old. Neve' thought to end me days in peace. Young face 'ung like a moon over me somewhere—somewhere—"

"It was in the vestibule," she reminded him gently, brushing her wet lashes with the back of her hand. "You crawled there after your fall."

The good side of his face quivered slightly in what might have been an attempt at a smile. "Whoeve' would have thought that a littl' damosel like you'rn could chase old Kingsmill an' Cobby an' Hammond an' all the rest of 'em devils away."

"Who are they?" she questioned, puzzled.

He did not answer her, but darted a sudden, anxious look at her. "You ain' brough' nobody else into my house, have you?"

"I'm on my own," she said. "Only the doctor calls."

"I won' abide strangers ove' my doorstep." He was aquiver with agitation, which caused him to start gasping for his breath.

She put a cool hand on his brow and spoke slowly and re-assuringly. "I give you my word that no other stranger shall cross your threshold while I am in charge."

The restlessness went from him, his breathing became more regular. Soon he closed his eye and slept. She wondered about the men whose names he had mentioned, and she as-sumed that these were the shadowy figures who peopled his troubled mind when he had talked and shouted during the long night hours and paced up and down the attic floor, and she was glad to know that her presence had somehow ban-ished his particular hell.

In the weeks that followed, his power of speech improved a little more, but that was to be the limit of his advancement. Christmas came and went. The splints were removed from his leg, but it was wasted and quite stiff, and Harriette did not need the doctor to tell her that even if it had healed in a healthy way the patient would never walk again.

Strangely Mr. Hardware was singularly content, showing not the slightest sign of regret at his continued immobility, the lack of power in his limbs. Although he remained mentally adult, in other ways it seemed to Harriette that he had become very much as a young child, regarding his bed as a safe haven of tranquillity, knowing that in it he was watched over and protected. Neither he nor she ever spoke of her leaving him. His trust was complete and absolute, and she felt irrevocably committed to the care of him, as she would have done had she rescued a bird with a broken wing or a kitten taken too soon from its mother. She had discovered that he needed to be reassured of her presence at all times, but most of all he wanted her at his bedside whenever he woke.

As a result she was rarely out of the house, although some-times she did take a brisk walk around the Square, bundled up against the snowy weather, whenever she could be sure that he would sleep without waking for a while or when the lawyer made one of his occasional visits to discuss some private matter of business with him.

There was a new governess next door, a thin, middle-aged woman who looked as though life had browbeaten her and she felt the cold. Sometimes on her walks Harriette would catch sight of the woman with Phoebe and Caroline, who deliberately ignored her, their noses stuck up in the air. But on one occasion Caroline, dawdling behind the others to crack the ice of a frozen puddle with the heel of her boot, happened to glance up and see Harriette a few feet away from her. They looked at each other.

"I received the letter you left in the schoolroom for me, Miss Mead," Caroline said awkwardly.

Harriette smiled. "I'm glad I was able to set your mind at rest about the dragon. No more nightmares?"

Caroline gave her a smile in return. "They've quite gone." There was a pause before she spoke again in a rush. "I did like you, you know. Very much. You were the best governess we ever had. That's why I picked the rose for you that day —I tried to tell you how I felt without letting Phoebe know."

Harriette stared at her. The rose! She had pressed it and kept it, believing it to have been a token of love from Robert, and she had treasured it since as a souvenir of the time when his feelings for her had been real and true.

"It was a kind thought, Caroline," she managed to say. She had suffered the final blow. It had been a severing with the past. Caroline had cut her free, but the pain was excruciating.

"I'd like to speak to you often," the child went on, unaware of the shattering effect her words had had, "but Mama has forbidden it. I overheard her say that you have a liaison with Mr. Hardware, whatever that means, as you did with Robert—"

"Caroline!" snapped the governess's shocked voice from the portico. "Come in this instant! You know you are not allowed to address that person!"

With a gasp of dismay at being spotted in conversation Caroline bolted off to dart past the governess and into the house. Harriette slowly continued her walk, her face white, a healthy anger that such slander should be uttered against her burning through her. The sky above was darkening ominously with the threat of more snow to come, seeming to emphasize the bleakness of her existence with the last trace of love she had known taken from her.

"Who are Kingsmill and Cobby and Hammond?" Harriette inquired one gloomy February afternoon when she was tidying Mr. Hardware's pillows. She had often wondered about them since he had mentioned their names on that first day when he had shown some signs of recovery.

"Why do you ask?" he gasped, his hands atremble on the coverlet. "Have you see'd 'em?"

"No! Of course I haven't seen them," she said quickly. "You mentioned their names once. That was all."

His eye went fearfully toward the door. "Have you heard 'em then? Are they moving about in the attic?" His breath began to rasp. "Dear God! Are their ghosts not laid yet!"

She felt a chill of horror at his words and held his hand tightly between her own in an effort to quieten him. "No! I've heard nothing! Nothing! Neither shall you! You told me yourself that my presence had banished them! They've gone!"

He looked fixedly at her for a few moments while he struggled for breath, and her clear, candid gaze did not falter. Gradually he relaxed, but he was much shaken by the incident. "I know you wouldn' lie to me, Miss Harriette. I know."

He was exhausted. She smoothed his covers and left him to sleep, vowing to herself that never again would she question him about anything even remotely connected with the past. She left his door open, knowing he always wanted to be certain she was within call, but before she crossed the landing to go downstairs she looked over her shoulder at the flight that went up to the attic. What dark secrets lay hidden there? It occurred to her that she knew very little more about Mr.

Hardware now than she had on that first day in his house. Once he had mentioned being born in 1727 on the day that George I had died, which seemed to have been considered an ill omen, and on another occasion he talked a little about his childhood, saying he had had good parents and grown up in a Hampshire hamlet. But how he had made a living or amassed enough money to buy his London residence she had no idea, and she had never asked him anything until this day and what a mistake that had been!

She watched him carefully during the next few days to make sure he had suffered no ill effects, but all went well and he appeared to have forgotten the incident. At times, boxed in the house alone with her patient with no one else to talk to, waves of depression assailed her, which she found hard to shake off. She welcomed the diversion of paying for goods delivered and exchanging a comment on the weather with whichever tradesman it was who came to the door. Sometimes she saw post being delivered to the Warringtons' house and she wondered if any of the letters were from Robert. She no longer yearned after him, having closed the door on that chapter of her life when she had thrown the carefully preserved rose in the fire, but it was with a forced brightness that she re-entered the sickroom, her talk sounding garrulous to her own ears, aware of her movements being brisker and more lively as though physical activity could keep all dreary thoughts at bay. Sometimes she had the feeling that Mr. Hardware was not unaware of her state of mind, but she always dismissed the notion, convinced that he did not remember the day when she had put her head on his bed and wept out her love for Robert and its passing.

She kept the sickroom fresh by opening the window whenever the weather permitted and putting flowers by the bed. When the snowdrops were over she waited until the first spring flowers showed amid the undergrowth in the garden and brought in colorful bunches of the tiny blooms. She was in the basement kitchen arranging some primroses that she had found when a clanging bell told her that someone was at the front door. It could be Mr. Bellamy-Jones or perhaps the doctor. Nobody else ever rang that bell.

Quickly she removed her apron and, smoothing a few wispy tendrils of hair into place, she hurried up to the hall to answer it. Benedict Sutcliffe stood at the doorstep. A look of amazement washed over his face. "Good day to you, Miss Mead! Have I come to the wrong house?"

"No, indeed," she replied. "I've simply changed my place of employment from next door."

"Has old Hardware taken children under his wing to need a governess?" he inquired on a note of continued bafflement.

"I'm no longer a governess. Mr. Hardware has been very ill. I've become his nurse and his housekeeper."

"Have you indeed! Then without doubt I may expect a more civil welcome than that which I have received in the past." He made as though to enter the house, but she took a step forward and barred his way.

"I cannot invite you in, sir. Mr. Hardware will see nobody."

Benedict Sutcliffe's handsome face darkened. Before she realized what had happened he had clapped his hands onto her waist and with a swoop she was lifted up and set aside, her cry of protest ignored. He had entered and shut the door before she was able to make a move.

"Now," he said with angry impatience, "perhaps you would be good enough to tell Mr. Hardware that he has a visitor to see him."

Fury took possession of her. Never before, she thought, had she had to deal with such an arrogant, high-handed individual.

"Kindly leave this house at once, sir! I gave Mr. Hardware my solemn word that I would let no one enter his home, and you have made me break that bond!"

He frowned, uncomfortably aware of what he had done, but determined not to retreat. "Forgive me. I will accept full responsibility, and you shall not be blamed. But it is on a matter of utmost importance that I wish to speak—"

A shout resounded somewhere on the third floor. Harriette threw him a blazing look. "There! You see! He has heard you! Go! Oh, please go!" She turned about and started hurrying up the stairs. "I'm coming, Mr. Hardware! Don't be alarmed!" At the top of the flight she glanced back. The intruder stood solidly with feet apart at the foot of the stairs.

"Tell him that I don't intend to leave until I have spoken with him!" he told her grimly.

Mr. Hardware's shouts were louder. She threw herself into his room and found him almost out of bed, his arms flailing. "Someone's down there! No one comes i' my house! Sen' 'em away! Sen' 'em away!"

There was a purplish flush to his face that worried her, and she tried to soothe him, pressing him back against the rumpled pillows. "A gentleman called wishing to see you. I told him to leave. There is nothing to be upset about. He simply stepped inside before I was able to stop him. Lie still for a few minutes while I see him off the premises, and then I will come back to you."

He was gasping and coughing. "Who is i'? Wha's his name?" When she told him he gave a choking roar that made her fear he was about to expire in the same breath. He raised himself up from the pillows and caught at her arm with surprising strength. "Sen' him away, for mercy's sake! Tell him to go back to where he's come from! I'll neve' go there again! Don't let him drag me to tha' house!"

She thought she understood his strange terror. When even the King himself was incarcerated from time to time for periods of insanity it was quite possible that Mr. Hardware with his odd, nervous behavior had been confined to an institution earlier in his life, perhaps even Bedlam itself, and had lived in fear of being returned to it, for all were dens of horror. It would explain why he had refused to receive all callers, trusting nobody. At the present moment he was suffering under the delusion that Mr. Sutcliffe had come to take him back to such a place. It was an absurd assumption, but a sick man could not be expected to reason logically. With difficulty she disengaged herself from his grasp, for he was clinging to her as though to a lifeline. "Nobody shall take you anywhere. I swear it! You're in my care and I'll protect you. Lie quiet. Breathe deeply and slowly. There's no need to be afraid."

He submitted to her coaxing and sank back again, but the wild distress in his eye was pitiable. Before leaving the room she took down from the wall the blunderbuss that hung there, and for the first time she sympathized with his decision to reside on the third floor, seeing that it gave a distinct advantage over any intruder on the ground floor or at basement level.

She descended to the second floor and came to a halt at the head of the flight down to the hall where Benedict Sutcliffe stood waiting. Calmly she aimed the blunderbuss at him.

"Get out!" she ordered. "Go back to where you came from! That was the message I was instructed to give you!"

Incredulously he stared at her, setting his hands on his hips. "Put that archaic weapon down. It could be dangerous."

"Mr. Hardware believes that you've come to drag him back to some madhouse! He's been a little disturbed in his mind, but he's not mad. I'll not have him tormented by your being in his house a moment longer! No wonder he's kept his home barred to you!"

"What is all this talk of a madhouse?" he exclaimed in angry bafflement. "Have you lost your wits in this dreary place? What business do you think I'm about, pray?"

She took a few steps down, still aiming for his heart. "All that matters to me is that Mr. Hardware has consistently refused to see you and he wants you gone! Now get out—or I'll fire!"

A smile touched his lips. To her dismay he started to mount the stairs, calling her bluff, confident that she had no intention of pressing the trigger. "Since there seems to be the strangest confusion over the reason for my calling, I think I'd better explain things myself to Mr. Hardware!"

A great sob broke from her. She knew the effect it would have on the old man to see a stranger enter his room. "He's ill! You shall not fright him and bring about his death!"

She lunged with the blunderbuss in a threatening way, intending only to make it appear that she intended to fire, but the trigger responded to the slight extra pressure of her crooked finger. The noise of the explosion deafened her momentarily and the violent recoil of the weapon sent her reeling back off balance. Her heel missed the stair and she went slithering down on her side, the blunderbuss clattering ahead of her.

When the choking smoke cleared slightly she looked up to see Benedict standing over her, unharmed, but furious. He reached down and yanked her to her feet. "You are certainly prepared to go to great lengths to help your employer play his game of hide-go-seek! If the man is as ill as you say, I regret my intrusion! I'd hasten no man to his grave, but I'll be back when he is better! Have no doubt about that!"

She did not wait to see the door close after him, but gathered up her skirt and raced back to the sickroom. There she found the old man racked by pain in the throes of a new attack of apoplexy. She loosened his nightshirt collar and propped him up, but did not dare to leave to fetch the doctor, for his eye remained fixed on her in mute appeal that she should not go from him, and she knew he was terrified of dying alone. Not until his eyelid closed in exhaustion was she able to fetch medical aid, but it was as she had supposed. Dr. Fielder informed her that nothing more could be done.

From that day she watched her patient sink rapidly into a state of weakness from which there could be no recovery. He spoke only in whispers and slept most of the time. Mr. Bellamy-Jones came and sat by his bedside, leaning forward to catch his client's words. Harriette, making tea for the visitor in another room, heard the rustle of documents and the scratch of a pen.

The following day the lawyer returned, and this time he was accompanied by a clergyman, the Reverend Halliday, who was shabbily dressed, but possessed of a bellowing voice with the aroma of ale heavy on his breath. To Harriette's surprise the lawyer asked her to remain in the sickroom and not to leave.

"Sit down, Miss Mead," he said, waving her back to the chair at the bedside. "This time you are concerned in the matter that we are about to settle."

"I, sir?" She took her seat again and waited.

The lawyer looked at her over his spectacles. "You have looked after Mr. Hardware faithfully and well. He would have died if you had not found him when you did, and you have been tireless in your efforts to make these last months a time of rest and peace for him. He is concerned that no gossip should linger on after his passing to taint your future in any way, and for this reason, as well as his desire to leave you with a roof over your head, Mr. Halliday is with me today. You see, Miss Mead, it is Mr. Hardware's last wish on this earth that you will allow him to give you his name in marriage."

She was deeply touched. Her gaze traveled to Mr. Hardware, who lay dozing while the momentous offer was being made, unable to keep awake for any length of time. It had been difficult to like him, for he was not the kind of person who drew affection from others, having that strain of hostile aloofness common to those used to a solitary existence either through choice or because of circumstances. Their relationship had been based on respect for each other, with trust on his side and a sense of responsibility on hers. She had looked for no reward for what she had done for him, grateful that he had inadvertently saved her from possible destitution, and with the wages she had received in payment she would be able to exist through the intervening period while she sought out another post of governess when the time came.

"Mr. Hardware," she said quietly, but clearly enough for the sound of her voice to make him rouse himself and look at her. "You do me much honor, but I have been glad to nurse you and—"

He interrupted her in a gasping whisper. "Marry me, Miss Harriette. Don' refuse my dyin' wish. Let me know that you will not let that earth-bound fiend ensnare me beyon' the gates of death."

Then she knew the true reason that lay behind his offer of marriage. From the moment she had taken charge of him she had given him the security that had somehow banished his strange delusions, but he was afraid that once he had parted from her his torment would return, and by making her his wife he would be leaving her as a bastion against all the forces of evil that he imagined might otherwise pursue him into the unknown. This was a request she could not refuse. He should die in peace.

"I will marry you, Mr. Hardware," she said.

The marriage ceremony was soon over. The gold ring from Mr. Hardware's little finger was her wedding band and it fitted perfectly. She heard his full name for the first time. She was Mrs. William Steele Hardware.

He died two nights later. Quietly. In the last few seconds he opened his eye and looked directly at her. "I saw you the day you arrived at the next house. Pretty as my fair Charlotte." Then with a long-drawn-out sigh he was gone. Somewhere up in the attic there came a muffled thump, almost as though a frustrated fist had banged the floor, but Harriette paid it no attention, although some part of her mind registered it without her being aware of it until later. Her thoughts at that time were full of thankfulness that in his last few moments Mr. Hardware's thoughts had been directed toward someone whom he had once loved. Perhaps his first wife. She doubted that she would ever know.

After the funeral Mr. Bellamy-Jones read her the will which had been drawn up the day before she had married Mr. Hardware. Harriette found that not only had she been left the house in Perbroke Square, but also another in the country village of South Bersted on the Sussex coast. In addition he had left her the contents of both houses, as well as a small amount of money, which added up to the sum total of his possessions.

When the lawyer returned a few days later, he gave her the keys to the South Bersted house, which had been kept with the deeds in a small tin box that he had brought with him to hand over to her. In it Mr. Hardware's will had been stored, together with all his other papers. The label told her the name of the residence. Bryony Lodge.

"Had Mr. Hardware no one else in the whole world?" she asked.

"Not a soul," the lawyer replied.

"He mentioned a woman's name just before he died."

"Did he?" The lawyer shrugged. "I know nothing of his life before he moved to London some years ago and asked me to handle his affairs. He was a secretive, cautious man, grudging with his information."

"I understand he moved into this house about five years ago."

"That is correct. He stayed longer under this roof than any other of the town properties he lived in before buying Number Eighteen Perbroke Square, and I must say that he became more eccentric and more of a recluse with every move." He dismissed the late Mr. Hardware as a topic of conversation and turned to his new client's affairs. "Have you formulated any plans yet? Naturally you will wish me to dispose of the Sussex estate. It's not large, as you heard from the will, and in its present neglected state I doubt whether it will fetch very much, but speaking frankly, Mrs. Hardware, you have not been left more than modest means on which to live, and although you can continue to live in this house, engaging two or three servants, it would be advisable to get rid of the country property as soon as possible. At present it brings in no income except a token payment of one shilling a year from the tenant who farms the land there, and although a more realistic rent can now be charged, I think you would find the whole estate more trouble than it is worth."

"In other words I cannot afford to own two houses."

"That is the case."

"I'm thankful to say that does not cause me any heartache," she said. "You see, as soon as I heard about the Sussex house in the will I decided to live in it. Perbroke Square has unhappy associations for me and I would not have stayed here anyway. Number Eighteen is the residence that I want you to sell for me, Mr. Bellamy-Jones. I intend to make a fresh start amid new people and new surroundings."

The lawyer raised an eyebrow. "You realize that the house

has been shut up for a number of years? It could be in a sad state of disrepair."

"Then I shall invest the money I receive from the sale of this property into restoring it." She glanced about her almost nervously. "I want nothing from this house. It can all be sold."

"There is not a great deal to sort out, I suppose. Mr. Hardware appeared to be a man of few possessions. But there is no need to make haste over anything. I will delay advertising that the house is for sale until you have made the Sussex residence habitable and are ready to move in."

She leaned forward slightly in her chair. "There *is* need for haste. I want to leave Perbroke Square as quickly as possible. Tomorrow!"

"Tomorrow?" he echoed in disbelief.

She nodded, avoiding his eyes. She could not tell him that since Mr. Hardware's death she had had the uncanny feeling that some alien presence was abroad in the house. He would think that she was letting her imagination run away with her, that she was getting infected by Mr. Hardware's fears. But it was not imagination that had made her go several times to the foot of the stairs leading to the attic, wondering why a cold draft, which had never been there before, kept sweeping down to chill her as she stood there.

"Perhaps you would be good enough to order a hired carriage for me, Mr. Bellamy-Jones," she requested. "It must be at the door by seven o'clock in the morning. It is a long journey to South Bersted and I want to reach my new home before nightfall." She rose to her feet. "I will show you how I have packed everything during the past few days."

The lawyer noted the box of the late Mr. Hardware's clothing, which his widow wished to be distributed to the poor. Every cupboard and drawer had been cleared, each piece of china packed in straw, and everything labeled. He could invite an auctioneer in the next day if he so wished.

Harriette picked up Mr. Hardware's gold watch. "I would like you to have this watch, Mr. Bellamy-Jones," she said, handing it to him. "I feel sure that Mr. Hardware would be pleased to know that you had a memento to remember him by."

It was a gold hunter. The lawyer was gratified, for it was a timepiece superior to his own and it lay heavy on the palm of his hand. "That is most kind of you, ma'am." He snapped it open and saw that it had stopped and the hands stood at two minutes past five. Was that not the time when old Hardware had died? Perhaps he was mistaken. He closed it and put it in his pocket. "Now I must take my leave of you. The carriage will be at your door at the hour you requested."

An anxious look flew across her face. "Can you not stay a little longer? I have not yet been up to the attic and there may be some of Mr. Hardware's papers or other documents stored there."

Mr. Bellamy-Jones had no intention of waiting while she explored a dusty attic, especially when it would reveal nothing, as he hastened to point out to her. "Everything of importance was kept in this deed box," he said, tapping it with a finger. Then he withdrew a step or two, intent on making his departure. "We shall be in close touch through correspondence, but I will visit you in Sussex if any matters arise that you wish me to deal with personally."

"I'm most grateful," she replied, resigned to the fact that he had not realized that she had wanted him to go up into the attic with her. Well, she could not make herself ridiculous and beg him to go up there with her. It was something she would have to do on her own. He was bowing over her hand.

"Good day to you, Mrs. Hardware. I wish you good fortune in Sussex."

She closed the door after him. Her first task was to finish her own packing and that should not take long. Afterward she would take a peep in the attics. The whole house was bright with the late-afternoon sun and she chided herself for her foolish misgivings. But by the time she had strapped down her trunk, leaving the traveling bag open to take her overnight things, the afternoon had clouded over and rain started to fall. Her first thought was that the Sussex roads would be like a mire, but her second was that with the going of the sun the whole house had become chill and dark.

Was there any real need to go up to the top of the house? She tried to tell herself there was not. As the lawyer had said, she would find nothing of importance. But if she did not explore the place, would she ever be able to banish the conviction that she should have gone for Mr. Hardware's sake?

Reluctantly she lit a lamp, not trusting an unshaded candle in case it blew out. Summoning up her courage, she moved in an arc of pale light up the attic stairs, thankful that the cold draft, which she had feared, was absent. Or was the attic too still? Holding its chill breath—and waiting! Firmly she drove these thoughts from her mind, telling herself that the absence of the draft meant that the wind was blowing in another direction, but that would not stop her from trying to find out where a loose slate or a crack in the brickwork was letting it through.

At the head of the stairs she came to a standstill and summed up her surroundings. They were planned exactly as in the adjoining property. In front of her were the tiny rooms, little more than cupboards, which were designed for use as storage space or servants' quarters, and of the two main doors the one on her right would lead to the room next to her old bedroom in the Warrington household, and the other would open into a large room corresponding to the schoolroom.

She decided to look in the smaller room first. With a swift movement she turned the handle of the door and flung it wide, uncertain of what she might see. But the room was empty of furnishings except for a large sea chest which stood by the dividing wall between the two houses. Immediately she understood that it had been the heavy lid crashing back which had sounded as though Mr. Hardware had been wielding a great hammer against the wall.

With a wry smile, remembering how alarmed she had been on a number of occasions next door, she crossed over to the chest and found it locked. Wondering what it contained, she drew back and looked at it. Brass-bound and battered, black with age, it looked as though it had followed Mr. Hardware about on his travels all his life. The key would be on his key ring in his bedroom, and she remembered noticing that one old key was larger than all the rest. After looking in the other room she would fetch it and open up the chest.

She went through to the other door, but drew her hand sharply away from the handle before she touched it. The icy draft was coming through the keyhole like a needle. It had been the slamming of this door which had cut off the unnatural chilliness that had descended into the rest of the house. It was in this room that she must search for the aperture that was letting the wind through.

Steeling herself, she opened the door and entered the cold room. The feeble lamplight did not shine far and she had taken no more than a few steps when her foot came in contact with something soft lying on the floor. With a sharp cry she stepped back and looked down. It was only a bundle of old clothes tied with a piece of rope which was frayed at the end, and a large card pinned to a coat lapel. Stooping down she turned it toward her to read the name written on it. *Thomas Kingsmill.* That was one of the names that Mr. Hardware had mentioned.

Something odd struck her about the way the bundle lay on the floor. It was an effigy! Setting the lamp down on the floor beside her, she straightened out the figure, which had been roughly made of sacking and stuffed with straw before being clad in an old coat and breeches with a tricorne hat and wig on its head. Then she saw why the head lolled when she touched it. The rope was a noose about its neck!

Slowly she stood up and lifted the lamp to look at the rafter above her head. It was as she had expected. Tied around it was the other end of the rope on which the effigy had swung until the continual draft and the resulting friction had frayed the rope through. Was the thump of the effigy's fall the sound she had heard that day when Mr. Hardware had died? Was it to this faceless effigy of Kingsmill—whoever he may have been!—that the old man had shouted night after night in the past?

How cold it was! There must be a broken pane in the window. The curtains across it were stirring in the draft. She moved briskly across to it and sent the curtains rattling back on their brass rings. The gloomy dusk blended with the pale light of her lamp, enabling her to examine closely the panes of glass, but none was missing or cracked. Then she heard the door close on the other side of the room.

With a wildly beating heart she whirled about and the light in her lamp went out as neatly as if snuffed by a finger and thumb. She did not cry aloud at the grisly sight that met her eyes, but a silent scream went through her and the lamp dropped from her shaking hands to the floor. The gray gloom had taken over from the black shadows that had hidden the other effigies which hung on various lengths of rope from the rafters overhead. It was as though she were standing amid a cluster of gibbets displaying their dreadful burdens. The names pinned on each effigy stood out at her. *Hammond. Jackson. Carter. Tapner. Cobby. Mills, the elder. Mills, the younger. Perrin. Fairall.*

As she stood there as though transfixed, the draft, which she now realized must be coming through a loosened slate somewhere in the roof, swept over her and around her, causing her collar to flutter and sending tendrils of her hair flicking across her face. The faint whining sound that it made was weirdly like that of a wind blowing bleakly across a heath, and all the effigies were on the move, swinging to and fro, round and about, in a macabre dance, the ropes creaking, the clothes flapping.

She began to edge past them back across the room, her arms taut and straight, her hands clenched, longing to escape and be free of that awful place. Then the effigy of Cobby swung out a little farther and the ragged lace under the coat sleeve brushed against her face like papery fingers. Her nerve gave way. She bolted for the door and hurled herself against the handle. It turned, but the door, although it rattled and shook, would not open. It was almost as though the draft was exerting pressure to keep it closed and her entrapped.

With her arms across her face for protection from further touch she dashed back to where she had dropped the lamp. Swooping it up, she hurled it with all her might against the window, thinking of no other way to release that draft before it became a whirlwind. The glass shattered into a shower of glinting shards. Only then did all become still again and the door opened to her touch.

Down in the Square, Benedict Sutcliffe, alighting from his carriage, looked at the lamp that had smashed down on the pavement in front of him, and then his gaze shot up to the jagged hole in the window at the top of Number Eighteen. But no face appeared to see if any harm had been done to any passer-by and his lips set grimly, his mind forming the suspicion that it had been aimed at him! He ran up the steps and created such a thunder with the knocker on the door that any listener might suspect he would break the door down if not admitted this time.

He was not kept waiting long. Harriette's face was chalk-white against the tangle of her dark gold hair, which was in disarray, and her mouth was soft and trembling. Concern for her well-being overcame his indignation over the lamp.

"Are you ill?" he demanded, giving neither bow nor greeting.

"No, Mr. Sutcliffe," she replied distinctly, although she spoke with some effort and a wary hostility rose in her eyes, showing that their last encounter was very much in her mind. "I'm well enough."

He was unconvinced. She looked as though she had received a severe shock of some kind, but she had made it plain that it was no concern of his. "The lamp—?" he said, leaving the question in the air.

She glanced toward it. "I hope it didn't frighten your horses when it—er—fell out."

His horses! He swallowed his indignation. "How is Mr. Hardware's health?" he inquired on a terse note. "Improved sufficiently to enable him to receive me now, I trust."

"He's dead," she said in a voice drained of emotion.

"Dead?" he echoed.

She nodded. "The funeral has already taken place. I advise you to contact Mr. Bellamy-Jones about your business, whatever it may be. Mr. Hardware did not take me into his confidence and I'd be unable to help you in any way. Now you must forgive me. I have much to do. I'm leaving this house in the morning."

She made to close the door, but his hand shot out and held it. "Where are you going?"

She raised her eyebrows slightly at his impertinence. "Out of London. Goodbye, Mr. Sutcliffe."

The door closed in his face, bringing the brass knocker within an inch of his nose before he could utter another word. Irritably he turned to retrace his steps to his carriage. He would have to come to grips with that dubious lawyer, who had looked blandly at him in the past, saying that only Mr. Hardware could deal with any queries, for he himself had no authority to intervene. Benedict gave a sigh, wondering who had inherited from Mr. Hardware and whether the person or persons concerned would be more amenable than the recluse who had stubbornly refused to see him.

Settling himself back against the velvet upholstery of his carriage, he wondered where Harriette Mead was bound. Well, he would find out. There were ways and means, and he had no intention of losing trace of her. He had not shown the sharp anxiety that had pierced him at her announcement that she was going away, but he had known in that instant how important she had become to him during their brief encounters, hostile though her attitude was to him now. He could remember in accurate detail his first sight of her. There she had been, perched high on a cart seat beside the driver, her fine features framed by her bonnet, her remarkably beautiful eyes looking directly into his for no more than a few seconds, and yet such was the impact made on him that he had turned to look back after her, seeing her alight from the cart, glance upward at Hardware's window, and then move gracefully up into the portico of the neighboring house. At the time it had been no more than a fascinating glimpse of a pretty girl unconscious of her own magnetic charm. Little had he realized how enchanted he was to become from that moment forth.

Harriette stayed leaning against the door until the last rumble of the carriage wheels had faded in the distance, enervated by the shock of her experience in the attic followed by the fear that Benedict Sutcliffe might again try to force an entry, not believing her word that Mr. Hardware was dead.

Wearily she lifted her head from where it was resting against the panel and made her way slowly down to the basement kitchen. There she searched among all the contents she had packed up until she found a stout carving knife. It glinted in her hand as she returned with another lamp up the stairs to the attic room, collecting on her way a chair on which to stand.

The almost monumental stillness of the effigies was, for a moment, almost as unnerving as their wild gyrations had been, but resolutely she dragged the chair forward and with gritted teeth she mounted it to reach up and cut down those motionless figures.

It took several trips to carry them downstairs to the garden. It was dark and cheerless, no star able to penetrate the black clouded sky. With sticks and paper and old wooden boxes she built a base for the bonfire, on which she piled the shapeless bundles in their ancient clothes. When she put a flame to it the fire leapt, and the air became filled with the smell of burning straw and woolen cloth and old wigs.

Not until nothing remained but glowing ashes did she go back into the house. In the basement kitchen she took a drink of water for her smoke-parched throat. There she sank down at a table and rested her arms on it, the half-emptied glass in her hand. Her head drooped forward and she felt herself sliding into a deep sleep of exhaustion.

# Six

"ANYTHING ELSE to be put on the traveling chariot, ma'am?"

Harriette, who had seen her brass-bound trunk carried out, as well as a hamper of provisions and a box of bedclothes and other necessities, was on the point of shaking her head when she remembered the chest in the attic. She could not leave it behind unopened. It would have to go with her.

"Yes. In a room at the top of the house you'll find a chest."

It was heavy. The coach driver and the groom enlisted the help of the young clerk who had been sent by Mr. Bellamy-Jones to collect the keys of the house from her. Harriette, who had taken her seat in the chariot, felt it dip and sway as the chest was pushed and shoved aboard.

The clerk came to the window. "Mr. Bellamy-Jones wishes you a safe journey, Mrs. Hardware."

She acknowledged the message with a quiet word of thanks. Then the chariot jerked forward with a shout from the coachman, and it was on its way so speedily that there was no time for her to take a last look at the house and its neighbor, both of which had been instrumental in changing the whole course of her life. She sat back, watching Perbroke Square slide past the windows and give way to Piccadilly and then the Strand. The Thames lapped blue and gray and silver in the early daylight as the chariot crossed the bridge at a spanking pace. There was every sign that the weather would remain fine and dry throughout the long journey, and Harriette felt that she should take it as a good omen of all that lay ahead of her. But the nightmare experience she had been through was still with her. Like a burden that would not be shaken free.

The journey went well, with few mishaps, in spite of the poor state of the roads. The sun had set, leaving the sky tinged with rose and gold when finally the chariot drew near to South Bersted and Bryony Lodge. Harriette gave the name of the house some thought, wondering if in the autumn ropes and wreaths of bryony abounded in the area, hanging like pearls of orange, crimson, yellow, and green amid spike-leafed foliage. It was said to have a black root, blacker than night itself. "Black as evil" was the phrase used in her part of the country.

Suddenly a shout came from somewhere on the road ahead. "Halt! I wish to speak to Mrs. Hardware!"

She knew that voice! Benedict Sutcliffe! But how did he know her to be Mr. Hardware's widow? The chariot came to a standstill with a creaking of springs and harness. Leaning forward, she let down the window as he came riding up to her, strong and graceful in the saddle.

"Good evening, ma'am." He swept off his hat. "After leaving you yesterday I went to see Mr. Bellamy-Jones, who gave me the surprising news of your marriage to the late Mr. Hardware. From him I also obtained your new address, and I departed from London without delay in order to be certain of arriving home in plenty of time to offer you hospitality after your journey."

"I don't understand," she said in bewilderment. "Do you live in the parish of South Bersted?"

"Within a stone's throw of the church. We are not exactly neighbors, you and I, for your house lies half a mile away along a lane that turns off by the signpost, but I have land that runs parallel to yours for some distance before my woodland outstrips it. I invite you to spend this night—and as many after as may suit your convenience—under my roof. I cannot let you go straight to Bryony Lodge. It has been shut up for years. It could be full of rats."

She had not thought of that possibility. Dust and dirt and

cobwebs were what she had expected, and she had decided that after the chest and her luggage had been unloaded she would have a light supper out of the provisions she had brought with her and find a spot to bed down for the night. But rats!

"There is a hostelry somewhere in the district," she said hastily. "I can stay there."

"Indeed you shall not!" he said on a note of authority. "It is fit only for hackney coachmen, peddlers, and the like. No place for a lady on her own. With your permission, ma'am, I will inform the driver of your chariot to follow me to your new destination."

He did not wait for her answer, but drew his horse away, and she heard him issuing orders and directions. What an extraordinary fellow he was! Arrogant, stubborn, strong-willed, and yet kindly too. He had expressed a genuine concern at her shocked appearance yesterday, and now, after traveling through the night to get home, he had ridden out again in the evening to wait for the appearance of her chariot when he could easily have posted a servant on the spot.

The chariot had not gone far when it drew level with a cluster of some twenty or more appalling hovels, comparable only to the worst streets she had seen in London. Most of the windows, which had never known glass, were either blocked up with lumps of turf or boarded up with old timbers to keep out the weather, and the thatch had worn so thin on some of the roofs that they were patched with sacking and sheets of old metal. A woman, fetching a wooden bucket of water from a well, stopped and stared at the passing vehicle, her face gaunt, her arms showing pitifully thin. Some children, filthy and in rags, who had appeared in all directions at the sound of the horses and wheels, rushed forward to beg, holding out their hands, causing the driver to shout and swear, pulling on the reins in fear of some of them falling under the clopping hooves. Moved by the sight of their pallor and emaciated condition, Harriette fumbled in her purse and threw out a handful of coins.

Almost at once Benedict wheeled his horse around and came alongside the open window through which she was gazing after the children, who had been joined by the woman, scrambling about after the money at the roadside. "You're generous indeed! That money will buy them the first good meal that they've eaten for many a day."

"Does no one care for the poor in this district!" she exclaimed compassionately.

"Those people are on the parish. The winter months are hard on them. Many die of cold and chest fevers."

"It is a disgrace! Such hovels are not fit to house swine!"

"I agree. In fact, I'm most eager to talk about these properties to you later." With these words he left her and rode forward to indicate with his whip the direction that the driver was to follow.

Some other dwellings came into sight, but these were cottages with well-tended, neat vegetable gardens. Leaving behind a tavern with the swinging sign of a white horse, the chariot followed a fork of the lane bearing to the left, past a smithy and some bow-fronted shops on one side and thatched cottages and more elegant houses on the other. The spire of a church stood tall above the treetops against a dusky sky from which the last tint of the sunset had faded, and a few yards further on a gateway appeared in a high flint wall. The driver drove through it in Benedict's wake to follow the sweep of a graveled drive which encircled a wide lawn with a central flower bed. The house itself was large and gracious, warm with lighted windows, its entrance enhanced by a porch around which roses would cluster in profusion in the summer. On the left lay the coach house and stables, and a door in a tall flint wall gave entrance to a private walled garden and an orchard beyond, although this she was to discover later. At the moment, looking out at the front door outside which the chariot had stopped, Harriette was only conscious of a welcoming atmosphere about the house. Almost as if it had been waiting for her.

"Welcome to Holly Wood House," Benedict said, swinging

open the chariot door to hand her out of it, having left his horse to the groom who had come running forward.

"You have a delightful home," she commented, entering the hall with him. The walls were striped silk, and stem-legged furniture held some fine pieces of porcelain. Through the open drawing-room door she could see a fire glowing to take away the chill of the evening.

"It was my grandparents' residence," he explained, handing his hat and riding crop to a footman, "and I was fortunate enough to inherit it some years ago." With a little sweep of his hand he indicated the presence of the housekeeper, who had come forward, neatly attired in black striped with purple, her fichu as snowy as her cap. "Mrs. Morgan will show you to your room."

"This way, madam," the woman said.

Harriette followed the housekeeper upstairs to a large and comfortable bedroom which in daylight would look out on the walled garden. Firelight danced on the rose-patterned bed hangings and across the carpeted floor.

"I will send a maid to attend you, Mrs. Hardware," Mrs. Morgan said, about to withdraw.

"Wait! One moment, please!" Harriette said quickly. The efficient domestic arrangements of this obviously well-run house had brought home to her how much at a loss she would be the following day when she moved into Bryony Lodge. No doubt it was due to tiredness from the journey, but she no longer felt able to face alone the stupendous task of putting a dirty, neglected house to rights. Mrs. Morgan might be surprised at being questioned about the availability of local labor for hire, but she would know better than anyone where it was to be found.

"Yes, madam?" The housekeeper waited politely.

"Tomorrow I'm moving into a house that has been closed up for years. Bryony Lodge. Do you know it?"

Astonishment and curiosity showed briefly in the woman's eyes, but she was too well trained to make any comment. "I do indeed."

"I was wondering if you knew of three or four village women who would be willing to clean and scrub the place throughout."

Mrs. Morgan seemed pleased that she had been asked. "Leave everything to me, Mrs. Hardware. The maids in this house are all local girls, and each one has a mother or an aunt or some other female relative who would be glad enough of the work. What time do you wish the women to be at Bryony Lodge?"

The matter was soon settled. Then the maid came and unpacked all that Harriette needed for one night. After washing away all the dust of travel Harriette put on her blue gown and arranged her hair with wispy tendrils curling down on either side of her face.

It was pleasant to descend the stairs to the appetizing aroma of a dinner in preparation, which escaped from the kitchen when a servant passed through the baize-lined door. She found Benedict waiting for her in the drawing room. Two glasses of Madeira had been poured out in readiness, and he handed one to her and took up his own.

"I must tell you that I'm exceedingly grateful not to be pushing my way through curtains of cobwebs at this moment," she said shyly, sitting down on the yellow silk sofa. It seemed strange to her that after clashing at each of their meetings they should be chatting together in such entirely different circumstances and on amicable terms.

He seated himself in a wing chair opposite her, settling back in it in a manner that suggested he was well used to its comfort, and he swung one long booted leg over the other. "Cobwebs, spiders, dust and dirt, and the rest of it will be there in abundance at Bryony Lodge, I fear. It has been closed up as long as I can remember."

"What is it like?" Her voice rose slightly on a sanguine note. "Is it small? I had hoped to find a little house."

He held his glass reflectively against the firelight as though studying the color of the wine, his lower lip pursed. "Small, no. But not large either, for that matter. It's much older than this house, which was built about seventy-five years ago. Yours dates from the early seventeenth century, I should say."

Hope still did not desert her. "Is it flint? Thatched perhaps? It will need rethatching without delay, I suppose."

"No. It's gray stone," he said abruptly, his gaze switching back to her, "and a slate roof that is covered with creeper—at least it was all those years ago when I used to climb the wall while on visits to my grandparents and steal apples from the deserted orchard."

"You haven't seen it recently, then?" she inquired bleakly.

"The high walls and the overgrown trees and shrubbery hide it completely from a lane that leads to Hammond's farm just beyond it. He will be your nearest neighbor, and the less you see of him the better."

"Hammond?" she echoed. "Surely that's the name of the tenant who rents the farmland that belonged to Mr. Hardware. Ezekiel Hammond! That was it."

He gave a brusque nod. "He's as wily a villain as it has ever been my misfortune to meet. As the local squire and magistrate, it is not only my concern that law and order should be maintained in this village, but I also consider that I have a duty towards the welfare of those that live in it. This is where I hope you will be able to help."

"I? In what way?"

He put aside his glass and leaned forward. "Bellamy-Jones told me yesterday that in future I must approach you first on any matter concerning the Hardware estate, which leads me to believe that your late husband bequeathed everything to you."

"That is correct."

"Then the time has come for me to explain my apparent harassment of William Hardware. It took me a long time to find him and had nothing to do with a madhouse. Bellamy-Jones was extremely uncooperative, and it was through no assistance of his that I eventually traced Hardware to Perbroke Square. You see, I wanted Hardware to take up his responsibilities in the village again after decades of shirking them. As far as I can discover, no fault can be laid at his door regarding his care of what he owned when he resided in Bryony Lodge, but after he left it everything was allowed to go to rack and ruin. Those wretched hovels, which you saw for yourself little more than an hour or so ago, are on the land that is rented out to Hammond, and I don't doubt that when Hardware lived in the village they were quite weather-tight little dwellings. Due to Hammond's neglect they have not only become places unfit to house swine, but in addition there are persistent outbreaks of fevers and all kinds of disease. The families who live in them are under Hammond's thumb. He expects them to work in his fields at wages even lower than those paid to the average farm worker, which is pitiable enough. One spring there was some rebellious show of dis-content. A few stones were thrown through the windows of Hammond's farmhouse, and a hayfield was set on fire. But he promptly laid off everybody and took on jobbing laborers from outside the district, and those of his tenants whom he did not drive out spent a winter of starvation."

Harriette saw again the faces of the starving children and without further thought said, "How terrible. What do you want me to do?"

He thumped a fist on his knee. "Give Hammond notice to quit your land and lease it to someone who'll do essential re-pairs to those properties, or rehouse the poor wretches on a better piece of land where they can at least grow a little more for their own needs."

"I will do that gladly!" she answered readily. "Mr. Bel-lamy-Jones did advise me to change my tenant at the earliest convenience for financial reasons, but I should do it anyway after what you have told me, even if Hammond had been paying a hundred pounds instead of a shilling a year."

"What!" Benedict exclaimed in astonishment. "A shilling a year for all those acres of land! Was Hardware out of his mind?"

"I really have no idea why such an extraordinary agree-ment was made," she said, adding impetuously, "but if you'll be kind enough to let me have paper and pen I'll write that letter to Mr. Hammond now."

He beamed his approval. "I cannot tell you how much I appreciate your swift action in this matter."

"Have you anyone in mind who might like to take over the land at a more realistic rent?" she asked, crossing to the bureau which he had opened for her.

He placed the quill pen in her hand as she sat down. "Would you consider me a suitable tenant?" he inquired with a grin. "Or, if you wish to sell, I will buy it from you, for it most conveniently lies parallel to my own acres."

"I believe I should prefer to sell it to you," she said, smiling, "but naturally I must have time to think it over." Suddenly she felt exhilarated and important, knowing what it was to have power and position for the first time. She was her own mistress. Never again would she have to run at another's bidding. Never again would she be banished to an attic room. Already she had been greatly blessed by the chance to put right a long-outstanding wrong. She had much to be thankful for. Turning her attention to the sheet of paper before her, she wrote the address of her future home at the top of the page. *Bryony Lodge. South Bersted. Sussex.* Underneath she wrote the date. *The fifteenth day of May 1809.* "Now, Mr. Sutcliffe, perhaps I may call upon your legal mind to assist me in the correct wording of this notice to quit."

"With pleasure!"

He stood over her, one hand resting on the back of the chair. When the letter was finished she shook the sand on it to dry the ink, and folded and sealed it.

"There!" she said, handing it to him. "Let us hope that the village will become a better place as a result of it."

"I have no doubts at all, ma'am!" He rang for a servant and gave an order that it be delivered to the Hammond farmhouse at once. She wandered back to stand in the firelight and take up her glass of Madeira again.

"I feel very foolish now that I know the reason why you made such determined efforts to see Mr. Hardware," she said. "I was truly a Medusa at the gate, but even so I did what was best for him—even to marrying him on his death-bed."

"I gathered that from the lawyer. I'd like you to tell me about your days in Perbroke Square," he said quietly.

Briefly she described the circumstances that had caused her to take charge of the old man, but she carefully avoided all reference to Robert. That was a closed chapter best forgotten. "Now I'm sure you understand," she continued, "how it came about that I could not grant you admission. Mr. Hardware had long since become a recluse, and only the past really existed for him. He had no interest in the present, and having once given instructions to his lawyer on how his estate was to be handled he would not want to be bothered by any suggestion of change."

"Surely that's a true indication of his character," Benedict replied, topping up his own glass from the decanter, since she had refused any more with a little shake of her head. "I put it to you that he had been a completely self-centered man all his life."

"I cannot hold entirely to that theory," she said thoughtfully. "He suffered much anguish of mind, which cried out for pity. And," she added, remembering Mr. Hardware's last whispering of a woman's name, "I firmly believe he knew love once and lost it."

At that moment a manservant announced that dinner was served. Benedict led her across the hall into a dining room that was softly lit, the wallpaper dark red and hand-blocked with gold. Over asparagus soup, local lobster, pigeon pie, and Southdown lamb they kept to lighter subjects, and she discovered that he could be most entertaining, having a keen wit that set her laughing. When he begged that they should be on Christian name terms with each other she saw no reason to refuse him and they drank a merry little toast together. In a singularly happy frame of mind she returned with him to the drawing room, where they drank coffee out of blue-and-gilt porcelain cups. The conversation returned to the subject of Bryony Lodge.

"My housekeeper could take over the appointing of staff

for you," he suggested. "She knows all the local families, and will find maids for you who will be honest and conscientious—"

Harriette interrupted him. "Oh, I have already consulted her about extra cleaning help for the first few days."

"Good. You can leave it all to her. Simply make a list. I advise two or three menservants at least. I don't anticipate any trouble from Hammond, but it will do no harm to let it be known that you have adequate male protection in the house and out of it. How many outdoor staff do you consider having? A coachman, two grooms, and a couple of gardeners?"

She was amused. "You are under a misapprehension as to my means, Benedict. Mr. Hardware left very little money and no possessions of any value. Until the Perbroke Square house is sold, or I have possession of Hammond's farmland to do with what I will, I must tread very carefully indeed. What funds I have must be devoted to making Bryony Lodge habitable. I intend to make do with one maid."

"That is not sufficient! You must have a trustworthy manservant as well!"

She eyed him curiously. "Hammond would not dare to harm me. You said that yourself. Yet you are anxious, I can see it. Are you reluctant to tell me the true nature of the man? Is he given to violence in drink perhaps? Or has he an ungovernable temper which might lead to some attempt to abuse me for turning him off the land?"

He was taken aback at her perceptive probing, but with a shrug he resigned himself to putting the facts before her. She was no foolish miss to be easily frightened, and since she seemed to think the presence of a manservant at Bryony Lodge unnecessary, he must convince her otherwise.

"There have been certain unsolved crimes in this neighborhood which have pointed very strongly to Hammond. But none will bear witness against him. They fear for their livelihood or the roof above their heads, or even their own personal safety. So you see, it is only reasonable for you to take all safeguards."

She was not alarmed by his remarks but inclined her head in sensible acceptance of his argument. "I will employ one manservant then. If only to settle your mind. Her tone was dry, but although he eyed her sharply her expression remained bland and unchanged.

"I suspect you still take my advice somewhat lightly, Harriette," he retaliated, "but ruthless men are involved in the smuggling that is taking place along this coast, and we know that brandy, tea, lace, and tobacco are being brought in from France all the time. We simply cannot discover where the contraband is unloaded and stored before it gets carried inland over the Downs. Sometimes horses get stolen to carry extra loads—I've lost a couple myself. My groom was knocked unconscious before he could catch a glimpse of his assailant, and other men have been most brutally beaten up when they've dared to defy the smugglers either by trying to protect their masters' property or their own."

"You think Hammond is the ringleader?"

He gave an emphatic nod. "I'm convinced of it, but so far it's been impossible to get any proof. In my hearing he has dared to boast of having smuggling in his veins. His father was John Hammond, a local man of Bersted, who was one of the notorious band of smugglers known as the Hawkhurst gang. He was tried with others of them at Chichester assizes and was executed at a rope's end soon afterwards. You've gone pale! It was not my intention to frighten you!"

John Hammond! She had never heard that name spoken before, but into her mind had leapt an image of a swinging effigy bearing that surname pinned to its coat. She had not considered that there might be any connection between Ezekiel Hammond and the effigy, for it was a common enough name, but it was impossible not to consider links between South Bersted and John Hammond and Mr. Hardware. Had the effigies been of long-dead smugglers of whom her late husband had once gone in fear?

"I'm not frightened," she assured Benedict truthfully, "only somewhat startled. In what year was John Hammond put to death?"

"It was in 1749—if I remember correctly."

Reckoning up quickly, she decided that Mr. Hardware would have been about twenty-two at the time. "Tell me about the Hawkhurst gang," she requested. "Not coming from the south of England I have never heard of them before."

"Have you not? Well, I suppose that is not surprising. It's ancient history, even in these parts, but being concerned with the law, I read up details of the trial at Chichester with interest some years ago." He got up from his chair and went to a bookshelf. Taking down a heavy volume, he flicked through it as he reseated himself, and he found the chapter that he wanted. "Since you are interested, I must get my dates right. Ah! Yes! It was in January 1749 that the bodies of two of the smugglers, John Hammond of Bersted and John Cobby of Sidlesham, were hung in chains at Selsey, where they had often landed their smuggled goods."

"*Two* of the smugglers," she said with emphasis. "How many more of them were there?"

"It is impossible to say exactly." He placed the book open and face downward on the table beside his chair. "The Hawkhurst gang boasted of such great numbers that on one occasion they went into pitched battle under their notorious leader, Thomas Kingsmill, against the militia at Goudhurst in Kent—"

"Kingsmill!" she echoed, all doubt wiped from her mind as she recalled with an inward shudder her foot kicking against that fallen bundle of rags on the attic floor in Perbroke Square. Those effigies—every one—had represented members of the Hawkhurst gang!

"—They terrorized that particular county in the southeast as well as Sussex," Benedict continued, "and they penetrated Dorset and Hampshire too. Often they rode openly in bands of a hundred men or more, and in the most brutal—and sometimes unspeakable—manner they dealt out vengeance to those local people who failed to cooperate with them. It often happened that villagers would take flight, leaving their homes and property to the marauders."

She was sitting stiffly on the sofa, unaware how tightly her hands were clasped. "How was the gang finally brought to justice?" she inquired, low-voiced.

"In the end they overreached themselves—in their daring as well as in the foulness of their crimes. It came about through the capture by revenue men of one of the smugglers' cutters, which was bringing in a great quantity of tea, as well as brandy and rum, from Guernsey. The smuggling crew escaped in a small boat without being taken, but the smuggled goods were impounded in the customhouse at Poole."

"That is in Dorset?" she checked, wanting to be certain of every detail.

He gave a nod. "The smugglers, who afterwards had the audacity at their trial to say that they were only reclaiming what was theirs, broke into the customhouse at Poole one night soon afterwards, and made off with the tea. In a kind of triumphant cavalcade they rode back into their own territory, seen by hundreds of gaping villagers on the way. A reward for information was offered by the authorities, and some months later a rather simple shoemaker of Fordingbridge, named Daniel Chater, expressed himself willing to give evidence of having seen the Hawkhurst gang with the tea when they had stopped to drink ale in his village and water their horses. It was therefore arranged that he should travel with a customhouse officer, William Galley, to make a statement to a Justice of the Peace, Major Battine, who resided at Stansted, near Rowlands Castle in West Sussex, not far from here. It was a Sunday in February—St. Valentine's Day, to be precise—when the two men rode into the village of Rowlands Castle and stopped to take some refreshment at the White Hart inn there—little knowing that they had stepped into one of the strongholds of the Hawkhurst gang!"

"What ill fortune!" she gasped.

"It was indeed. The landlady, a Mrs. Paine, sent one of her sons to alert the smugglers, and several of them came to the inn. It did not take them long to suspect what was afoot, and under the pretense of friendship they made the two men drunk. More than a little drunk themselves, the smugglers went through the customs officer's pockets and found the letter that told them Chater was going to lay evidence against them, which could bring them all to a rope's end. Now begins the worse part of the tale."

"I'll not faint," she said somewhat defiantly, as if fearful he might change his mind about continuing the account. "I want to hear it all."

"Galley and Chater, lying befuddled by ale, were most cruelly spurred about the face by one smuggler, named William Jackson, and then they were carried out to a horse, roped together on it, and led away. I have to tell you that once there was no danger of their cries being heard the smugglers whipped them viciously, ignoring their cries for mercy. So weak did they become that they fell under the horse, which meant that they were knocked about the head by the horse's hooves at every step that was taken. After a while the smugglers set them up on separate horses, making threats of throwing them down a well when they came to it, and all the time the whipping continued. It was on a slope of the Downs that Galley fell from the horse and broke his neck when he hit the ground. Although the poor wretch was not dead he was buried in a hole that they dug for him." He paused, seeing that she shuddered. "Harriette, I think—"

"Go on!" she prompted, almost angrily.

"Chater was eventually thrown down a well, but only after the most savage torture. The smugglers had left Rowlands Castle with their victims on Sunday afternoon, but it was not until late Wednesday night or early Thursday morning that stones were hurled by the smugglers into the well to silence Chater's last groans." Benedict leaned forward and put another log on the embers of the fire. "Eventually an anonymous letter named one of the smugglers who had been present. He turned King's evidence, and told the authorities everything they wanted to know." He picked up the book again and consulted it. "The trial took place in January 1749 at Chichester. William Jackson died in prison before he could be hanged, but the others—"

"When was Kingsmill brought to trial?" she asked quickly.

"Some months later. His whereabouts and that of two of his most vicious henchmen, William Fairall and Richard Perrin, were given away by the same smuggler who had turned King's evidence at the earlier trial. He stood witness against them too. Kingsmill was defiant to the last, threatening the witness that he would hound him to his grave, and answering back when judgment was passed and the hope expressed that the Lord would have mercy on the condemned men's souls." Benedict read a line from the page. "*'If the Lord has not more mercy on our souls than the jury had on our bodies,'* Kingsmill jeered, *'I do not know what will become of them!'* The three of them were hanged at Tyburn." Benedict closed the book and got up to return it to the shelves. Then he stood looking down at her with a smile. "Why on earth did we let ourselves get launched onto such a grim topic on this, your first evening in my home. I fear you will suffer some nightmare if we do not find some way to bring the color back into your face. A game of backgammon, perhaps?"

She relaxed, letting the horror of the tale she had heard recede from her. At least she knew something now about the Hawkhurst gang. It was to be hoped that she would never have to hear them mentioned again, for although she was no wiser as to why Mr. Hardware had hung effigies of them in the attic, at least she knew something about the ghosts from the past that had plagued him in his old age.

Benedict set up the backgammon board, but Harriette soon found that after her long journey that day she was too tired to concentrate. He saw this, and put out his hand to still hers, which held the container with the dice. "You are wearied by all the miles you have traveled since dawn," he said considerately. "Let us leave this game until tomorrow."

"I am ready to retire," she admitted, sitting back in the chair. "But the game will have to be postponed a little longer than that. Tomorrow I shall be moving into Bryony Lodge."

He made a sweeping gesture of protest. "But you cannot possibly move in until the place is clean and tidy. I want you to stay here for at least two or three weeks while everything is made ready for you—"

She interrupted him. "Oh, no! I don't want to sound ungrateful when you have been so kind, but you must understand that Bryony Lodge will be the first real home that I have ever known, and I want to be there to put it to rights in my own way."

His eyes narrowed on a glitter of mingled amusement and approval. "You're as stubborn as you are proud, Harriette. We're two of a kind, you and I. I look forward to our courtship. It promises to have more than its full share of excitement for both of us."

She stared at him in astonishment, rising to her feet. "Our courtship?" she gasped. "I must remind you that you haven't set eyes on me more than four times before this day!"

He grinned widely, coming to stand very close to her. "You kept count too, did you? I find that encouraging. I'm also glad that you made no coy and mawkish reference to being recently widowed, which I realize must have been a marriage in name only. I find your honesty and your candor intensely refreshing, for as you must have gathered over the past months I'm a man who likes to speak his mind. You're a beautiful girl, Harriette."

A beautiful girl. The words set off echoes in her heart. Robert had said that to her, not in ringing tones of admiration but in a soft, persuasive whisper, his hands caressing her, his breath warm in her face, his mouth seeking hers. It was too soon to associate love with anything but pain and sorrow and anguish and she wanted nothing more at the moment than to settle in her own home and find peace and comfort and solitude.

"I must be honest and tell you that I'm in no mood to be courted," she replied firmly, "and in view of what you have said, the sooner I leave your house the better. I'm grateful for your kindness to me, I regret that I showed you much hostility in the past, and I trust that we shall enjoy friendship now. Tomorrow I shall move into Bryony Lodge, no matter what state it is in. So I'll bid you good night—and thank you again for your hospitality."

She made a move toward the door, but he stepped in front of her. "You're wrong, you know."

She arched her brows in puzzlement. "Wrong? What about?"

"About your present mood." His gaze traveled over her face, as if he could never look his fill of her. "But for the time being you imagine that Bryony Lodge will give you the happiness and security you seek. For some reason that I cannot understand you don't completely trust me yet. Do I represent a threat to your new-found freedom?"

Perhaps he did. She wasn't sure. But she did know that he must learn that she would not be browbeaten into anything—least of all love. And what did she really know of him? Practically nothing! He could be a smuggler himself for all she knew. He wouldn't be the first gentleman or the first magistrate to lead a double life. Even his interest in getting possession of her land might have ulterior motives. Angrily and sadly she considered how cautious and suspicious Robert had made her of this man, who was laying siege to her as though she were the most remarkable creature that had ever crossed his path.

He took her silence for his answer. "There are many kinds of freedom," he said gently. "I'll never crush your bright free spirit. I'd give my life first."

"You assume too much!" she protested almost helplessly, her eyes luminous with anxiety and perplexity. She wanted only to escape from his disturbing presence.

"I think not." His tone did not change. "I've never seen a girl more in need of love and protection. Your eyes speak for your heart. Have no fear, Harriette. I can be patient if you wish it and it seems that you do."

With relief she nodded. "I'll be gone early in the morning. A village carter will remove my trunk, the chest, and the rest of my belongings as soon as it can be arranged."

He answered her with a characteristic explosion of wrath.

"Damnation to your carter! Do you have to make your eagerness to be rid of my company always so obvious? Your goods shall be transported in the same carriage that takes you to Bryony Lodge, no matter how early you choose to depart! In the meantime, sleep well. But do not imagine that you have made me change my mind in any way. I mean to have you, Harriette! Have no doubt about that!"

In her room she dismissed the maid who would have helped her to undress, wanting to be alone. Sitting down at the toilet table, she regarded her reflection uneasily. Did her eyes really give her away, revealing depths of emotional longings that she was not consciously aware of herself? Was it true that she wanted more than a haven in which to seclude herself? But surely only someone attuned in perfect harmony to another could decipher such inner shades of hope and despair. Did such an empathy exist between herself and Benedict? If it did she could not see it yet and indeed recalled his overbearing ways. All that was uppermost in her mind at the present time was an overwhelming longing to enjoy the freedom of complete independence which Mr. Hardware had bequeathed to her.

Getting up, she crossed to the window and held back the curtain. Somewhere to the west under that star-studded sky Bryony Lodge awaited her. Not until she had met her destiny there could she give any thought to love.

She frowned slightly. Why had that conviction suddenly laid hold on her? And why had a feeling of fear accompanied it? As though whatever it was might swallow her up, and her reaching out to love had come too late to fill her poor cold heart!

With a shiver she let the curtain fall back into place. Suddenly she dreaded the morrow. But she was committed to leaving Benedict's home and it was too late to draw back now.

# Seven

IT WAS A COLD, DAMP MORNING with heavy clouds when Harriette emerged from Holly Wood House and stepped into the waiting carriage. Breakfast had been served to her in her room, and she had seen no sign of Benedict, who, she assumed, must still be abed, for it was barely eight o'clock. With a rumble of wheels on the graveled drive the vehicle bore her away, and soon the village was left behind.

Bryony Lodge was no great distance away, as Benedict had said, but it stood in an isolated spot surrounded by woodland. One of the grooms jumped down from the back of the carriage to take the keys from Harriette, and unfastened the padlock of the gates, which were tall and rusty, entwined with ivy. With difficulty he thrust open one of them, but in a single glance it was easy to see that no horse or vehicle could get through the wild tangle of undergrowth that had smothered the drive over the years. His companion came to the carriage window.

"Mr. Sutcliffe warned us that it'd prob'ly be like this, ma'am," he said. "On his instructions we've brought a scythe and a chopper. We'll 'ack a path through—it'd take too long to prepare it for the carriage."

"Very well," she said.

She sat watching the two men set to work, but after a while she became bored and increasingly impatient. Getting out of the carriage, she paced up and down for a time. When they reappeared, hot, dirty, and in their shirt sleeves, it was not to her that they came first, but stepped aside to have a muttered word with the coachman, who in turn came to her.

"It might be best, ma'am, if you 'ad a look at the 'ouse afore the grooms move your possessions into it."

"I'm prepared to find it in a state of disrepair," she said, but her expression was anxious. "The roof has not fallen in, has it?"

"No, ma'am. Not as bad as that."

"Then there's nothing more to be said on the matter. Tell the men to start unloading. I'll go ahead."

She went through the gates, seeing out of the corner of her eye that the coachman shrugged expressively to the grooms as if to say he had done all he could to dissuade her from entering. Steeling herself for the worst, she set off along the space that had been hacked and trampled down for her along a drive that must have been gracefully curved and sweeping before the undergrowth and the weeds took over. Brambles and twigs snatched at her long skirts, and she saw how the house had come by its name in days gone by, for bryony was everywhere, let loose again to run riot as soon as the gardeners had all departed. Black bryony. That was its true name, because it was said that the roots were black as night. Black as evil!

She pressed on up the drive, tugged her skirts free each time they became hung up on thorns, the grooms following her, each with a piece of her baggage on his shoulder. When the house finally loomed into sight she came to an abrupt halt, momentarily overwhelmed by the wild wave of despair that assaulted her, and she fought down an impulse to turn tail and run back to the carriage and Holly Wood House. Its state of repair was no worse and no better than she had expected, but there was a bleakness about the house that was chill and unwelcoming. Built of gray stone, it was much more sprawling than she had thought it would be, parts of it dating back to the seventeenth century with ornate pilasters and an elaborately carved porch, which was approached by a flight of steps. A few slates were missing from the roof, but otherwise it looked sound enough, although a thick creeper had taken over and snaked down the walls to cover the upper windows with closely woven tendrils. The very fine lower windows, which were deeply inset, had a curiously blind look, being shuttered from within, and a number of cracked and missing panes gave a distorted reflection of the purple-shadowed day. A narrow forecourt had been taken over by weeds and tall grass, and of the two tall marble urns which flanked the stone steps up to the entrance, one was green with lichen and the other lay toppled and smashed on the ground.

It was all so different from the simple country house she had hoped for, having pictured in the beginning a residence little more than a cottage with a small garden that she could put to rights herself. Never had she imagined Mr. Hardware owning such a once-grand edifice, or—now that she had seen the place—ever living in it, which he must have done at some time.

The first thing that struck her as she entered was the sad, depressive atmosphere. She told herself that any house left empty for a long time would have the same chill, tomb-like air. On the flags of the hall the tap of her heels resounded uncannily. Through a coating of dust the tall pier glasses reflected her as she went to the foot of the stairs and turned to look about her.

She could see through an archway into a long drawing room, and on the other side one set of double doors was closed and another set was just ajar. No dust sheets covered the furniture, a fact that struck her as being extremely odd, and whoever had closed up the house had omitted to pack away the candelabra and a few other silver objects, which had been left to tarnish to a black-bronze that would need hours of polishing to restore to brilliance again. At her feet lay an old glove where it had been dropped and forgotten, and nearby was a darkish rag, which on closer inspection showed itself to be a cravat of ruffled lace that had turned brown and discolored by dust and time. It was almost as though both articles had been dropped in flight by someone intent on leaving the house and its contents as quickly as possible. Was she right in this assumption? Would she find the rest of the house left in a similar state?

Quickly she went under the archway into the drawing room. There she flung open the shutters, letting in the small amount of light able to penetrate the creeper overhanging the windows. Her gaze swept the room, and the dirt and decay made her heart ache for what had once been a beautiful room. Nothing had been covered up to protect it from the passage of time, everything festooned with cobwebs and thick with dust. Ashes of a fire were still on the hearth, and the hands of the ormolu clock had stopped at ten to four. But when? On what day? And how many years ago? Twenty? Thirty? Forty? It was impossible to tell.

She looked down at the carpet, seeing that here and there in the pattern moths had taken the petal of a rose and the curl of a ribbon. When she lifted up a cushion from the sofa the silk was rotten and it split, releasing a few feathers, and the spot on which it had lain revealed a pristine richness of yellow brocade.

Leaving the drawing room, she went on a tour of inspection, passing on the way the grooms who were setting down the second load of baggage and were going out of the house to fetch some more. Opening one set of double doors, she found another, smaller and more homely drawing room, but the half-open doors led her into a dining room where the dried remains of a meal for one person were still on the table, although the chair the diner had been sitting on lay overturned as though knocked backward in a hasty rising from the board. What had disturbed that solitary meal? What had made Mr. Hardware, for it could have been no one else, leave the house with such speed that he had taken no heed of what time would do to the house's contents and left it to rot away? No wonder he had cared nothing for the deterioration of his other properties in the village when his own home was of no consequence to him. Unless he had left the house in terror-stricken panic and wanted to have no more to do with it or anything connected with it!

In the kitchen she found stacks of unwashed dishes left to the spiders, and on the iron range was a pot that had once contained a stew of some kind that had long since dried and cracked into an almost fossilized state, and she supposed it had been a portion of that same stew which remained on the plate in the dining room.

"Mrs. Hardware!" One of the grooms was calling to her. She went back into the hall and found that the two men had carried in Mr. Hardware's chest. "Where would you like us to put this and the other trunks, ma'am? With the smaller pieces in the 'all or upstairs?"

"Upstairs," she said.

She led the way and discovered that there were four upper rooms and in addition there was an extra door, which she opened to find a rear staircase for servants. It mounted to the loft and descended to the kitchen quarters below. A quick inspection showed her that, unlike Perbroke Square, there were no separate rooms in the attic, but one large open space, some ancient truckle beds and other rubbish stored there.

Coming down the rear staircase again, she looked into each one of the bedrooms to decide which one she should take for herself. All had four-posters, but the largest in a north-facing room had satin hangings and a spread that had long since faded from deep blue to gray. She bade the grooms set the chest against the wall under the window, and when it was in place they went downstairs again to fetch up the rest of the boxes.

Opening the closet doors, she was amazed to find it full of clothes. There were a dozen gowns or more, beautifully preserved by their enclosure away from sunlight and dust. These must have been Charlotte's clothes! These had once belonged to the woman in Mr. Hardware's life! In cotton, silk, and damask they shimmered in pastel hues, some hand-blocked with carnations, violets, or roses, and others with a simple stripe. On the floor of the closet was a row of shoes and slippers in a small size, and on a shelf above the garments were two pompadour wigs and a collection of wide-brimmed hats, which would have been worn over frilled caps. Harriette was sure she would find a box of those lacy fripperies some-where.

They came to light in a drawer, together with night shifts and undergarments of finest cambric. What had Charlotte been like, Harriette wondered. Fastidious, without a doubt, for everything lay neat and unrumpled. Also her taste had been impeccable, for it was obvious that it had been she and not Mr. Hardware who had chosen the furnishings of the house.

Reluctant to disturb with her presence a room that seemed almost to be still occupied, Harriette chose another for her-self and directed the carrying of her possessions into it. The absence of anything in the drawers and closet suggested that it had been furnished for the use of guests, or perhaps to await the arrival of a baby. Had Charlotte and Mr. Hardware had a child? There was so much she did not know.

Before the grooms left she opened her traveling writing desk and wrote a note to Benedict's housekeeper, asking her to find at least two more willing and able women to help clean the house, and the men departed, closing the door be-hind them and leaving her alone in the house.

She glanced at her fob watch. The first of the cleaning women and the laundry woman should be arriving within the hour. In the meantime she could make a start by open-ing the windows and letting in as much light as possible. To save time she had put on her most workaday dress when she had got up that morning and had no need to bother her head about whether it became soiled or not.

She found throwing open the windows a difficult task, sometimes having to push with all her strength, and upstairs she tugged at the creeper, pulling down pieces of it. Finding it impossible to break off some of the tougher tendrils, she turned to her luggage to take a large pair of scissors out of her sewing basket, and as she knelt to rummage through for them she experienced the odd sensation of not being alone.

She straightened her back, the scissors in her hand, her heart thumping. Something or somebody had moved out on the landing. She was sure of it. Slowly she rose to her feet, and she went soundlessly to the door, which stood ajar. With a lightning sweep of her hand she sent it crashing back as she darted out onto the landing. But there was nobody there. At least, nobody that she could see. At the same time something brushed against her face.

She panicked. Part of her mind told her it had only been a tendril of her own hair waving in the draft of the open wind behind her at the time, but the smell of that unseen presence was in her nostrils, chill and foul like the stench of death.

She flew down the stairs and, stumbling on the last stair of the flight, almost hurtled onto her face. But wildly regaining her balance, she continued making for the front door, which she seized by the handle and hauled open. And then she screamed out as if she had lost her wits, not expecting to find her way of escape blocked by a tall figure.

The red-faced, burly man in the steeple hat who stood on the doorstep, his hand raised to thump the knocker, was as startled as she was by the abruptness of their meeting and his bushy brows lifted in astonishment at her scream, hastily stifled.

She spoke first, a trembling hand pressed against her chest. "Your pardon, sir. I had not thought to see anyone when I opened the door."

"So it appeared," he snapped grimly.

"I'm Mrs. Hardware," she said, recovering herself. She had taken a dislike to the stranger and wished him gone. "What is your business?"

To her dismay he stepped inside, apparently taking her query as an invitation to enter. His high boots were muddy, his clothes rough and coarsely spun and not very clean, his neck cloth crumpled and begrimed. His small eyes, set bead-like above bags of flesh, darted curious glances about the hall before his gaze settled on her again, animosity and anger in his expression.

"This is my business, madam!" he retorted, flapping in her face the letter she had written only the evening before under Benedict's direction. "What is the meaning of it, pray?"

This then was Ezekiel Hammond, son of the smuggler whose effigy she had so recently burned on a bonfire. "I believe I made my meaning clear enough, Mr. Hammond," she said, not flinching before his aggressive glare. "Your tenancy of my land is at an end. I have seen for myself the terrible state of the cottages that you took over from my late husband, and I intend to see that they are repaired and made fit to live in. What's more, the rag, tag, and bobtail labor that you have brought in to farm the land has been another cause for dispute and trouble. In future local people shall have the local employment, which is their right."

He thrust his pugnacious face close to hers. "I had a gentlemen's agreement with Hardware that the land should be mine to farm throughout my lifetime, and then it should be willed to my son! I'd have had it in my name on paper if it hadn't been part and parcel of the Bryony Lodge estate, which was owned by the first Mrs. Hardware's father. She inherited it just before she died in childbirth, and then it became Hardware's, but he left sudden-like, and I never did get my document signed." He wagged an angry finger at her. "But that don't alter nothing!"

"Did the child live?" Harriette questioned, torn by this glimpse into a private tragedy about which she had known nothing until a few minutes ago.

"What? The child?" Hammond resented being dragged off the main thread of his discourse. "No. At least, no more than a day or two. Probably that as much as anything nigh sent Hardware off his rocker—seeing things and all that. But he never went back on his word to me about the land during his lifetime, and him being dead don't make a ha'porth of difference. The agreement still stands!"

"My late husband left everything to me, but I'm not bound by any verbal agreements made between you in his lifetime," she said coldly, "particularly as in your case you abused the privilege of the tenancy entrusted to you."

Hammond swore in his frustration, taking an angry pace one way and then the other as though scarcely able to constrain his feelings, his huge fists clenched. "I reminded the lawyer every time I paid my annual shilling about what had been promised me, in case the old fool went daft at the end. And daft he must have gone to wed a girl young enough to be his granddaughter!"

"Get out of this house, Mr. Hammond!" Harriette ordered. "I do not have to suffer your oafish insults!" She went to hold open the door, but he gave it a thrust that slammed it shut again, making her draw back quickly.

"I ain't finished! Bellamy-Jones was the name of the last lawyer I've been in contact with over the past five years. Did he say nothing to you about my claim?" He swore again most vilely. "If I'd been able to trace Hardware and tackle him face to face this would never have happened! But he was slippery as an eel. No end of lawyers he's had over the years, and never one would give his whereabouts away. I suppose he was always on the move, fearful of staying in any place long."

"If he had," Harriette observed perceptively, "I don't doubt you would have used your bullying tactics—whatever they were—to get more than the farmland he let you have and the sums of money you forced him to throw in from time to time before he escaped you! No wonder he took care to cover his tracks!"

Hammond's face darkened ominously. "I made no mention of force. That was your word, madam! Hardware was a man of tender conscience. He owed a straightforward debt to me. A debt that could never be fully repaid! Never!"

"I'm at a loss to understand what you're talking about," Harriette declared with some impatience. "What possible debt could be outstanding after such a long time?"

His tiny eyes narrowed incredulously. "You mean you don't know? He never told you? No more than he did his first wife!"

"I knew little of my late husband's affairs," Harriette was forced to admit, "but I believe him to have been an honest man and—as you so aptly put it—he did allow things to prey on his mind."

Hammond rubbed his chin thoughtfully, the bristles rasping. "Hmm. Then I'll tell you why you're duty-bound to follow your late husband's lead in continuing to lease me this land—and this time we'll have your mark and mine on a document that won't allow for no more quibbling. It was an action of old Hardware's that resulted in my mother being widowed and me being left fatherless while still a babe in arms."

Harriette folded her arms across her waist and clasped them tightly, realizing that she was about to have some of the mystery surrounding Mr. Hardware cleared for her, but she thought it best for the moment not to let Hammond know that she was aware of the nefarious trade that his father had followed.

"But luck hadn't quite deserted my mother and me," Hammond continued with satisfaction. "Some years later Hardware moved into Bryony Lodge with his new wife, and my mother recognized him. So I called on him. I was seventeen at the time and no sponger, but keen to earn my daily bread and make something of myself. Hardware let me take over the land and provided me with a plow and horses and cattle. Set me up right fine as a farmer, and I ain't never looked back. But," he added with emphasis, "it weren't no more than was due to me."

"It seems a great pity," Harriette said coldly, "that having found a benefactor yourself you did not in turn benefit those who became dependent on you for a livelihood as the years went by. Tell me, what was this action that deprived your mother of a husband and you of a father? Was Mr. Hardware the revenue man who brought him—and those other brutal murderers—to justice?"

His reaction was not what she had expected. His eyes expanded and he let forth an explosion of laughter, slapping his thigh and giving a heavy stamp of his boot. "That's the best I've heard in a long time! No, Mrs. High-and-mighty, he weren't! Hardware was one of the Hawkhurst gang himself! He'd have been strung up with my father and the rest of 'em if he hadn't turned traitor and saved his own skin! King's evidence, madam! He turned King's evidence!"

*128*

Her face had gone white to the lips with shock. William Hardware a smuggler too! No wonder he had been plagued with conscience in his later years, having betrayed his companions! And yet there had been no contrition in the shouting out at the effigies during those long nights of torment—only defiance and fear. Indeed, he had looked to her as a barrier against the past, wanting to go in peace to his end. There was so much more to all this! So much that she still did not know!

But one thing was startlingly clear to her. Mr. Hardware had thought to start a new life with his bride at Bryony Lodge, but fate had not finished with him. He was seen and recognized, and from that moment he had been given no respite. Young Hammond had come with threats to reveal the truth of his past association with the Hawkhurst gang, and Mr. Hardware, wanting desperately to keep it from his wife and from his new acquaintances in the village, had paid up and continued paying up until at last, after his wife's death, he had taken flight from the past once again, and had lived as a recluse and more or less in hiding for the rest of his days.

"So you see, madam," Hammond continued, his yellow teeth showing in a malevolent grin, "if you don't oblige me in the manner I've requested and get your lawyers to settle everything in my favor, it won't be long afore everybody knows that not only are you the widow of a smuggler, but he was a Hawkhurst man at that! Then you'll find that there won't be anyone among the local gentry who'll hobnob with you. In fact, I'd bet my last penny piece that it'll be worse than that. They'll not acknowledge your existence—you'll be shunned as the outcast that you are!" He laughed again, smoothing out the crushed letter, and then he held it between the finger and thumb of each hand, ready to tear it across. "Give me the word to scrap this piece of paper and we'll forget it ever existed. And when you've given me a better document to replace it you'll find I'll have forgotten that I ever knew your late husband!"

Swiftly she reached out and opened the door wide. "You

will vacate my land by the date stated. That is my final word on it, Mr. Hammond!"

He gave her a look of such black hatred that she was uncertain whether he could restrain himself from striking her, but she stood her ground, her gaze unfaltering, and to her relief he made a move to depart.

"You'll regret what you've done! You'd have been glad of a friendly neighbor, I'm telling you. Wait until you find out about this house! Why do you think nobody has wanted to live in it, eh?"

Benedict's voice spoke from the garden. "That's enough, Hammond. Be off with you."

Hammond turned and stumped down the stone steps. "You've been after depriving me of my rightful rents from my workers' cottages for years now, Squire. But now I've lost me land too! I'll fight it! I'll get lawyers and take the whole case to court! You'll see! I ain't beaten yet!"

When Benedict entered the house he found a pale-faced Harriette leaning with both hands on the newel post of the staircase for support. "Are you all right?" he demanded, rushing to her. "That villain didn't lay a hand on you, did he?"

"No," she said tremulously, "but it was an upsetting scene. What did he mean about the house?"

He took her firmly by the elbow and the wrist and led her into the drawing room, where he seated her on the dusty sofa. "There are always eerie stories about empty houses. In this case I suppose it was Hardware's hasty departure that gave rise to a lot of ridiculous suppositions. Not that I was born when he lived in Bryony Lodge, but as a boy I heard the servants tell tales of lights seen and voices heard. That was part of the attraction for me of climbing over the wall and having a look at the place. I even came by night a few times, and never did I see or hear anything unusual."

"There has never been a murder committed here, has there?" she inquired cautiously.

"No. I'd know if there had been. It would have been in the local records that I have in my possession. Why do you ask?"

She glanced warily over her shoulder toward the door. "I had a feeling of not being alone upstairs before Mr. Hammond came. There's something—wrong. Somewhere." She jumped nervously, startled. "What's that?"

"Only the arrival of the cleaning women by the sound of it," he said reassuringly. "I'll go along to the kitchen quarters and let them in."

"I'll come with you," she said quickly.

No fewer than six women and a red-haired girl came pouring in through the back door, and they had brought their own brooms and brushes and cleaning rags with them, not knowing what utensils would be available. They exclaimed at the dirt and the dust and the filthy cooking pots, and when they drifted into the rest of the house on a tour of inspection they threw up their hands at what they saw. Only the laundry woman wasted no time in idle discussion about all that had to be done. After a few businesslike words with Harriette she found a pair of steps and mounted them to take down curtains and bed drapes, sweep linen from the beds, and covers from pillows and cushions. She had a boy waiting outside with a cart, on which she piled the stuff in bundles, and he pushed off one load and came back for another.

Harriette, suddenly fired with enthusiasm, tied on an apron and started rolling up rugs to take them outside and beat them, leaving the floors clear for two of the helpers who had already heated some water on the range and were down on their knees with soap and scrubbing brushes.

Benedict, having lost track of her in the general hubbub, found her beating rugs amid clouds of dust in the garden, a cap covering her hair. Coming up unheard behind her, he snatched the beater out of her upraised hand, making her swing around toward him with an exclamation of amused surprise.

"Reconsider," he implored more on a note of command than appeal. "You cannot stay alone in a house that has already made you nervous when it is to be without curtains and every kind of comfort for the next three or four days at least."

Her eyes twinkled at him. "You are clutching that beater

so forcefully that I suggest you put it to good use on the rugs. There are plenty of other tasks I can do."

He hurled the beater to the ground. "Harriette!" he fumed in exasperation. "You heard what I said!"

"But I shall not be alone for more than a night or two," she answered, smiling at his ferocious frown. "Martha, the red-headed girl, has said she will work for me and will move her things in as soon as the servants' quarters in the attics have been made ready. What's more, her betrothed, whose name is James Willow, is in need of work, and he is to move into the rooms above the stables, which will make excellent accommodation for the two of them when they are wed. He is to be my gardener and handyman—and groom as well when I have purchased a horse and trap."

"I'll sell you a blue-painted gig that my grandmother used to drive and a nag to go with it!" he said promptly, knowing better than to offer them as a gift. "Seven guineas on the nail! Take it or leave it!"

She deliberated carefully. "Thank you, Benedict. That sounds a fair price. I know that the vehicle must be still serviceable and the animal strong and in good health. I accept your offer."

"Done!" He banged his fist into the palm of his hand, clinching the deal. He did not intend to let her back out of it when she saw what a pretty little mare he had decided she should have, which was worth four or five times the price he had asked. "All Sussex deals are settled over a drink. I cannot take you into the tavern with me, but I can ask you to take supper with me this evening. I have other guests coming," he added quickly in case she should reject the invitation out of hand. "It will enable you to meet some local people whose acquaintanceship you should find pleasing."

"That is most kind," she said. "I'll enjoy that."

"Then I shall call for you at seven."

"I'll be ready." Her glance went beyond him. "That must be James Willow! Forgive me. I must speak to him. I want him to start clearing the drive to allow space for vehicles to drive through."

She went darting off. Benedict saw that a shabbily dressed youth had come around the side of the house, staring with all the open curiosity of the country-born. The Willow family was known to him, people of honest stock, humbly placed, but hard-working, and he had no quarrel with Harriette's decision to hire the lad. What was more, James Willow was strongly built, and Benedict, seeing how easily the lad broke off a stout branch that was impeding Harriette's way, did not doubt that he would be able to deal well enough with any intruder who might dare to venture into the grounds. A few mantraps set near the walls would be an additional protection, and Benedict made up his mind to see about the matter.

Thoughtfully he viewed Bryony Lodge through critical eyes. It did no harm to let Harriette put the place in order. She needed something to do during the time of his courtship, which he intended to pursue no matter what she said. When she was married to him a good tenant could be found for the property, and out of the rents she received she could buy herself all the bonnets and gewgaws she fancied, which would help her to retain that feeling of independence that was so oddly important to her.

God! How he loved her. It was not sane to be so possessed by a passion that stretched beyond the tormenting fires of desire to a romantic, tender yearning to cherish her to the end of their lives together. He thought with relief of the marriage traps he had avoided, which had been set to snap by innumerable ambitious mothers who had considered him to be the catch of the district for their daughters. Suppose, enchanted for a while by some pretty face, he had committed himself and been truly ringed by that day when Harriette had ridden into his life on a dray cart with her eyes like fathomless golden-gray seas, full of unconscious promise, casting a spell on him. He had known many women in his thirty-odd years; some he had loved, some he had merely desired, but never before—not in England or during his extensive travels on the Continent during the Grand Tour and afterward—had there been one who had shown signs of being able to resist him when he'd made up his mind to have her. Conquests had always been easy for him, dating back to his student days at Cambridge, and even before that he'd had some amorous adventures. But until he'd seen Harriette he had never met any girl that he'd wanted to marry and be faithful to for evermore. He knew now that he'd been searching for her throughout all those years that had seemed so rich and full at the time. His grandfather had been a judge and was responsible for his having become interested in the law. Many times as a boy he had accompanied his grandfather to the courts at Chichester, and with his own nosegay to keep at bay the stench and infections of the prisoners in the dock, he had watched justice done. Often it was of a particularly brutal kind, but on the whole his grandfather had been a merciful man, and from him he had learned much that had proved invaluable in later years when he himself had become a magistrate and an administrator of the law. Until inheriting Holly Wood House he had lived most of the time in London, where he had enjoyed all the pleasures that the city and a wide social circle could offer, but since moving to South Bersted he had settled down to manage the estate and his business affairs, and take part in the quieter pursuits of the countryside. And now he, who had become wise and cynical and experienced beyond an ordinary man's measure, had been struck down like a love-sick boy—and he gloried in it. His only regret was that Harriette apparently could not see that they were destined for each other, and his very real fear of failing to win her affection, as he desired it, had been responsible for making him harsh-tongued and impatient with her on occasion, a fault which he must bring himself to overcome.

Flicking at the undergrowth with his riding crop, he wandered to where the outbuildings lay, separated from the rear of the house by a stretch of red-bricked yard, which had been taken over by groundsel and other weeds that stood waist high. He took a look inside the stable, wrinkled his nose at the stuffy odor of sour straw, and moved on into the empty coach house, his footsteps echoing hollowly on the tiles. Coming outside again, he decided there was something slightly different about the yard, but what it was defeated him.

Ah, well. Memory played tricks and a great deal of water had flowed under the river Rife's bridge since he had climbed trees in the house's orchard. With a shake of his head he retraced his steps and made for the spot where he had left his horse. But before he rode away he glanced back over his shoulder once again. Whatever had been changed there would come to him eventually. Like a sore tooth that a tongue cannot resist, the matter would niggle at him until he had solved it. At a dig of his heels his horse moved forward obediently and carried him away.

In the house Harriette met the laundry woman coming downstairs with a final armful of stacked linen, which had turned dark yellow with long storage.

"That's the lot, Mrs. Hardware," the woman said, the starched frill of her cap a-nodding. "I'll get the quilts, bed drapes, and curtains done first. Some of 'em will need a needle and thread before they're put back agin. There's a sewing woman in the village who'll do it all as neat as can be."

Harriette's expression became keenly interested. "Could she make me a new gown out of an old one, do you think?"

"I daresay she could." She went waddling on across the hall without stopping, and shouted back over her shoulder. "Me and the boy'll be going past 'er cottage in 'alf a tick. I'll tell 'er to nip over."

The dressmaker came promptly, a neat, bird-like woman with spectacles and tiny hands. She viewed the gowns that had been Charlotte's with a breathless admiration. "What beautiful garments! See how the panniers are embroidered! Nobody weaves fabrics of this quality any more! There's more than enough stuff in the skirt of any one of these to make you a gown in today's style, Mrs. Hardware."

"That is what I hoped," Harriette said, taking out one of rich green silk covered with tiny white rosebuds, which had originally been worn over a hoop that had jutted out over the hips. "Take this one first. I want it made on neoclassical lines, the bodice low-cut, and use the garment's ribbons to ornament the gathers under the bust." She put her head on one side, looking thoughtfully at the gown she held at arm's length away from her. "The sleeves should be puffed, I think. And very short. That is the fashion in London these days."

"Certainly, madam." The dressmaker pulled out her measuring tape. "It shall be done exactly how you wish. It seems to me that the lady who owned these clothes must have been very similar in height and figure to you."

"So I believe," Harriette said quietly. "The late Mr. Hardware told me that once."

It was almost half past six by the time the cleaning women departed, and Harriette was well pleased with their day's work. She had made them all a cup of tea before they left, which—had they but known it—was as much a luxury to her as it was to them, but Mr. Hardware had enjoyed a sip of tea from time to time, and she had brought the canister and what was left of its contents with her from Perbroke Square.

She sat for a while longer in the newly scrubbed kitchen and drained the last drops of the pot into her cup. When she had emptied it she put it with the others to be washed up in the morning and went to fill a pitcher of hot water to take upstairs and bathe away the toil of the day.

In the hall she caught sight of her reflection in one of the pier glasses. There was dirt on her face and apron, but it did not matter. The hard work had done her good, keeping her physically active, giving her no time to consider how much she disliked Bryony Lodge. But she was getting control of it and she must remember that. It had tried to frighten her early in the day, but it would not succeed again, because she was determined to turn this pile of bricks and mortar into a home, and eventually she would overcome her aversion to it. It was hers. She was mistress of it. For the first time in her life she was at nobody's beck and call. Independence was an intoxicating wine that she had never tasted before.

She was about to turn away from her reflection when her gaze became riveted in the glass toward the top of the stairs where the rays of the setting sun, penetrating the fanlight above the front door, had created a pattern of shadowed streaks against a rosy glow. There had been a sudden inexplicable glint of light. As though the sun had touched a brass button or the hilt of a sword. A mere flash, but she had seen it! She was certain of it. Somebody—or something—had been there on the landing. But all the cleaning women had gone home. There was no one else in the house!

She set down the pitcher, snatched up her skirts, and tore up the stairs. Reaching the wide landing, she stood panting, her glance darting in all directions. Not a corner existed where anyone could be concealed. No board had creaked. No door had opened or closed, not even that which led to the rear staircase, which had such squeaking hinges that she had made up her mind to get James to oil them at the first opportunity.

She should have been reassured, but she was not. There was an eerie atmosphere about Bryony Lodge that had plagued her for the second time that day. The sooner she could drive it away with open windows and summer days, the better it would be. In the meantime she must avoid letting her imagination play her tricks.

But she still looked warily about her when she came upstairs again with the pitcher of water and bore it into her bedroom, where the fragrance of lavender drifted from the bed, which had been made up with linen and blankets and quilt from her own bed in Perbroke Square. There she snatched off her working clothes and poured cold water from a ewer already placed there during the day and doused her face in it as though to shock away her nervousness. Only after that did she add the hot water and bathe herself from head to toe.

The dressmaker arrived half an hour later with the finished gown. Harriette was waiting in her petticoats, her hair brushed and gleaming and pinned prettily into place.

The gown fitted perfectly except for a very minor adjustment, which the dressmaker, who had brought needle and thread with her, put right in a matter of minutes.

"My! That suits you indeed!" the dressmaker said, standing back admiringly.

Harriette knew it did suit her. The rich green set off the creamy color of her skin and seemed to deepen the hazel color of her eyes. The dressmaker had skillfully fashioned a rose out of an inset of white satin in the original garment, and this Harriette fastened in her hair, where it glowed with its green silk leaf against her hair.

"Later on I should like you to alter some of the other garments for me," she said.

"Gladly, Mrs. Hardware," the dressmaker replied, much gratified at having been paid on the spot. The gentry usually kept her waiting for her money as though it were beneath their dignity to fork out for honest toil performed in their service. "I could take another with me now if you like."

Harriette hesitated, knowing that it would be an extravagance, but she was desperately in need of clothes, and at least the gowns would only be costing the price of remaking. "Very well. Take the lilac muslin."

The dressmaker departed with it over her arm. Harriette opened her trinket box and took out the pearl pendant on a gold chain, which had been her mother's, and she fastened it about her neck. Taking up a shawl, she left the room and went downstairs, having only a few minutes in hand before Benedict was due to arrive.

How different the house looked wiped clean of its dirt and cobwebs, and although it was not finished yet, the stale, rancid atmosphere, which had so alarmed her when she had caught a concentrated whiff of it earlier in the day, had gone. Instead there was a not unpleasing aroma of beeswax and soap and plate polish, and although the house had a naked look without drapes or curtains at the windows, there was a glossy gleam to the furniture in the candlelight and a mist of dust no longer dulled the satin sheen of the paneled walls.

She was glad to see Benedict when he arrived and there was no mistaking the flare of appreciation that showed in his eyes at the sight of her.

"You look lovelier than ever this evening," he said warmly.

Her spirits lifted and she basked a little in his admiration, realizing that she had been too busy all day to look forward to the evening, but now that it had come she was going to enjoy it.

"Do you know, I have not been to a social event in a private home for as long as I can remember," she confided as they left the house. "At least, not as a guest—only to keep an eye from a distance on my pupils when they were allowed to attend for a short time in order to be seen by everybody."

He paused, gathering both her hands into his, looking down into her eyes. "This evening you are the guest of honor, Harriette. Make no mistake about that! And everybody shall know it!"

She disengaged her hands, smiling. "Your kindness knows no bounds," she said, turning to get into the carriage.

"Kindness!" he muttered, getting in beside her. He rapped with his cane and the carriage moved forward.

They reached Holly Wood House with plenty of time to spare before the other guests arrived. She was struck afresh by the graciousness of his home with the candlelight glowing on bowls of spring flowers, and in the drawing room a bright fire danced invitingly. On the way she had told him all that Hammond had said to her that day, and the first thing he did was to take down the same book that he had referred to the previous evening and look up the facts of the trial again.

"Hammond must have been lying," he said, leafing through the pages to the section he required. "Hardware is such an unusual name that I should have remembered it, but there was no one of that name mentioned, I feel sure. Ah!" He had found the page. "There were two smugglers who turned King's evidence. One was William Steele and the other—"

"That is he!" She sprang to her feet from the chair where she had been sitting. "Not until I married him did I learn that his name was William *Steele* Hardware! He must have taken a new surname when he tried to put the past behind him!"

Before he could make any comment there came a ring at the doorbell, which meant that the first guests had arrived. "We will talk about him later," he said to her, "when everybody else has gone."

She nodded, and when he had put aside the book he took her by the hand and drew her to his side to present her to his guests as though she were already mistress of his household.

Benedict, as Harriette had expected, proved to be an excellent host, attentive to every one of his guests, lavish with his hospitality. She found herself much in demand, the gentlemen interested to hear she was the new owner of Bryony Lodge, the ladies eager to discuss the London fashions with her, obviously impressed by the style of her gown, and invitations to call came from every one of them.

It was after supper that the local doctor, an elderly man in an outmoded tie wig, came and sat with her.

"I knew your late husband, ma'am. I remember going to Bryony Lodge—um—many years ago. Thirty-five to forty, I suppose it must be."

Her whole face showed her interest. "What was Mr. Hardware like in those days? That was long, long before I was born. I only knew him in the last year of his life."

"Forgive me, ma'am, but that I cannot tell you. Um. I do not think I saw him—um—on more than five or six occasions at the most, and only a couple of those were professional calls. He was much distressed by his wife's untimely death—that I do recall. Never have I seen a man give way to such abandoned grief. I feared for his sanity. Not long afterwards he left the village. To my knowledge he never came back again."

"That is correct. Poor Mr. Hardware. To lose both a young wife and a firstborn child—"

"Ah, ma'am, but the lady in question was not young. More his age—say, forty years to his forty-five. Late in life to bear a child, but all would have gone well if she had not suffered some great fright, which caused her to tumble down the stairs from top to bottom."

"A great fright!" Harriette echoed. "What could it have been?"

He shook his head from side to side. "I was never able to discover. Mr. Hardware was incoherent in his grief, but I gathered they had had a visit from some old enemy of his from the past. Whether the lady was threatened or not I was unable to discover, but it seemed to me she simply missed her footing on the stair in some distress and was unable to save herself."

"Was any name mentioned?" she inquired.

"Of the intruder, d'you mean? Um. Yes. I do remember that. A Mr. Kingsmill. It stuck in my mind at the time, being the same name as that of a certain fiend who had been hung in chains at Goudhurstgore some years before the tragic accident at Bryony Lodge. But that name will mean nothing to you."

"On the contrary, Dr. Keane," she said, her heart palpitating at what she had already heard. "I know that Thomas Kingsmill was the leader of the notorious Hawkhurst gang."

He peered at her over his spectacles. "That is correct. The most wicked band of smugglers that has ever plagued our Channel coast."

"Tell me more about Kingsmill," she requested. "I know little about him, except that he was defiant to the end."

"He was indeed. But he had been a most villainous rogue throughout his twenty-eight years. No one knows the amount of wines and spirits, tea, and other valuable goods that he brought into the country, outwitting the revenue officers every time. He would lead a band of sixty to a hundred armed men openly on a raid, fearing no one. Any unfortunate villager who failed to cooperate or whom the gang suspected of cheating or trying to betray them was murdered most brutally. There was the case of that unfortunate carpenter at Yapton, not far from here, who, failing to surrender a bag of tea with the rest of the stuff he had hidden for them, was taken to the Dog and Partridge at Slindon and—um— whipped to death before his body was thrown into the pond at Parham. I tell you, ma'am, it was a blessed day for this part of the world when Kingsmill was finally taken and the Hawk-hurst gang broken up forever."

"I understand that two of the smugglers turned King's evidence over the murder of Galley and Chater," she said carefully, encouraging the doctor to talk on, "but Kingsmill was not taken then."

"That is correct. It was a few months later that one of those same two smugglers gave his whereabouts away. Kingsmill was most insolent at his Newgate trial, shouting at the judges and trying to intimidate the witnesses with the most dreadful threats of what he would have done to them. Finally he was condemned to death with two of his most notorious henchmen, but only he and the one called Fairall were hung in chains, and when the third fellow lamented that their bodies were not to be buried decently, Kingsmill laughed. '*We shall be hanging in the sweet air while you are rotting in your grave!*' Those were his very words."

She gave an involuntary shiver. "So he was never laid to rest."

"No, ma'am. More's the pity. There's an old Sussex saying in these parts that such evil is best buried deep as the roots of black bryony."

The old doctor was unaware that he had struck horror into her. Was it possible that William Hardware had imagined himself haunted by the ghost of Kingsmill? He must have had more than his share of threats from Kingsmill while in court. Had he taken his wife's death as proof of Kingsmill's vengeance? The shock of that particular tragedy combined with the constant harrying of Hammond for more money had finally put him to flight, and by hanging up that effigy of Kingsmill with the others he had tried pathetically to assert himself against the forces of evil that had continued to plague his mind. In the end she herself had come between him and that evil. Could it be that inadvertently she had drawn that evil toward herself?

"How—how do you know all this, Dr. Keane?" she asked in a shaky voice.

"I have—um—always been interested in the case—among others. Benedict and I have had many a long talk about crime and punishment. With smuggling still going on in these parts he is most anxious to bring the ringleaders to justice, but they continue to evade the revenue men."

Some other guests came up to sit with them at that point and the subject of smugglers past and present was dropped. But when the party began to break up, Harriette and Dr. Keane spoke to each other again about the Hawkhurst gang.

"It has been a great pleasure meeting you, Mrs. Hardware," he said, bowing over her hand. "I trust that my talk about that villain Kingsmill and the others will not give you the nightmares."

"I'm sure it won't, but I've a mind to go to the tavern in Rowlands Castle where the smugglers used to gather. I understand that it is not far from here."

"No, indeed. The lanes are poor and the turnpike leaves much to be desired, but you could ride there and back in a day without finding it too tiring. Would you allow me to escort you, ma'am? I admit to a curiosity about the Hawkhurst gang that never wanes, and I have never yet visited the White Hart."

"Thank you, Dr. Keane," she replied. "I should be glad of your company."

Benedict, turning from seeing the last guest out the door, came back to where she waited for him. "Did I hear you making an assignation with old Dr. Keane?" he teased, smiling.

"Not exactly," she answered, and went on to tell him about their conversation. "I should like to know exactly what threats Kingsmill issued against William Hardware at the Newgate trial."

"That should not be difficult to discover," Benedict said, "but it would take time to get detailed information of a trial that took place such a long time ago. I will go to Newgate the next time I'm in London and take a look at whatever records have been kept."

"You are good to me, Benedict," she said, rising to her feet in readiness to leave.

"Good to you!" he exclaimed. "Have you no measure yet of all I feel for you?"

"I am aware," she replied, "but I must remind you of what I said when you declared your intentions only twenty-four hours ago in this very room. It is too soon for me. We have known each other for so short a time."

"It's months since we first met!" he argued indignantly.

A smile quirked one corner of her mouth. "I was not

counting those earlier meetings, one of which was alarmingly hostile. Our true acquaintanceship started when you waited for me to arrive from London. That was yesterday, or had you forgotten? You promised to have patience, Benedict."

"That has never been easy for me."

"I understand that, but I have ghosts to lay. That is all I can say."

"Ghosts? What do you mean?"

"I'm not sure I know myself." She frowned pensively at the golden embers of the fire. "Bryony Lodge challenges me. Or does it threaten me? I don't know. Either way I must put it in order. Until I do I cannot give my mind to anything else—or my heart to anyone."

"At least tell me that there's nobody else in your life."

She turned to face him. She could answer him truthfully. Robert was no more than a painful memory which she would dwell on no more. Her heart was bound to no one. "There is nobody else."

"Harriette, my dear, dear Harriette," he breathed.

She saw then that he intended to kiss her for the first time and there could be no drawing away. There was so much love in his very aware eyes that she quivered inwardly, standing motionless. His arms enfolded her and his mouth descended to take hers in a kiss that proved to be of such passionate tenderness that almost without her realizing it her lips moved under his, and she clung to him, her body arched against his, her eyes tightly shut while she lost momentarily all thought of cold, dark Bryony Lodge and all its shadowed corners in the ardor of his kiss.

"Don't go back to that dismal place tonight," he urged, still holding her. "I told the housekeeper to leave your room as it was."

She shook her head, moving out of his arms. "I must go home. Have you a lantern I can borrow? I want the carriage stopped by the churchyard on the way back to Bryony Lodge. I'm curious to see a certain grave there."

"At this hour! Can't it wait until morning?"

"I'll go alone if you don't wish to come," she said with gentle mockery.

"I'll bring the lantern," he said with a resigned sigh.

The church stood black against the moon-gray sky. Benedict held the lantern high and its fitful rays danced over the ancient porch before moving on to follow Harriette as she made her way across to the gravestones on the west side of the church.

"Whom are you looking for?" he inquired, seeing how closely she peered at the ancient lichen-covered headstones, some of which had tipped to an angle.

"Charlotte Hardware and her baby," she replied, moving on to read another.

They found the tomb eventually in the southeast corner under trees that bent their branches low. Benedict held some of them aside for Harriette to push her way through.

It was enclosed on its own in a kind of cave woven by the dipping foliage, which was shot with silver in the moonlight. Harriette stepped onto the plinth on which the lichen-covered tomb rested, and leaned over it to trace with her fingertips the barely decipherable lettering. "*Here lies Charlotte, beloved wife of William Steele Hardware. Born 21st September 1732. Died 5th August 1772. Also their daughter Elizabeth, who graced this world for two days. Rest in Peace.*"

Slowly Harriette lowered her face and placed her cheek against the cold stone, almost as though she hoped that through physical contact all the compassion that she felt might penetrate the lid of the tomb to reach the long-dead woman who lay there with her child beside her. When she raised herself up again Benedict took hold of her by the elbow to steady her.

"I've learned more about William Hardware in the short time I've been in South Bersted than during all the months I nursed him," she said, walking at Benedict's side along the path that led them to the gates. "You remember I asked you if there had been a murder at Bryony Lodge? Well, there was in a way. That is, Mr. Hardware believed—according to

Dr. Keane—that it was a ghost from the past which was responsible for Charlotte's death." Then she told him everything the doctor had said.

"Does the knowledge that you were so nearly right disturb you?" he asked anxiously.

She considered carefully, "It does. I cannot deny it. But I'm gathering up my defenses. I feel that in the future I'll be able to tackle it, no matter what it might be, as I'll be forewarned by my own intuition when anything is amiss."

"You speak as though you have a battle on your hands!"

She gave him a deeply solemn glance. "I believe I have," she said simply.

When Bryony Lodge appeared beyond the thicket of half-cleared undergrowth they left the carriage and walked the last few steps across the forecourt and up the steps to the door. Harriette unlocked it.

"I left the tinderbox by the candles on a side table," she said.

He found it and lighted the candles. "There! That's better."

She saw he had closed the door after entering, but she had no intention of letting him delay his departure. Picking up the candelabrum, she lighted the short distance across the hall back to the door for him.

"I thank you for a most happy evening," she said. "I have been invited to call by so many kind ladies that I can see that once this house is finished I shall not have a spare moment on my hands."

"It was my joy to present you to so many of my good friends and their wives." He bent his tall head and put his lips to her cheek and to her hand. "Good night, my love."

She had shot the bolt on the door and fastened the chain by the time the rumble of the carriage wheels had disappeared down the drive. Protecting the candle flames with her curved hand, she went upstairs to her bedroom. On the landing she paused by the door of the room that had once been Charlotte's. What had she been like, that woman no longer young, who had in all innocence married an ex-smuggler and—murderer? Whatever his sins, William Hardware had suffered the torments of hell for them.

The moonlight showed her the chest where it had been placed by the wall. She had yet to open it and see what it contained. But not tonight. Tomorrow. She would open it up tomorrow.

She had barely entered her own room when she heard a sound which at first she took to be thunder, so low and rumbling was it. Crossing to the window, she looked out, thinking to see clouds gathering, but the night was as perfect as ever. As she stood there listening the rumbling died away again.

Puzzled, she began to unfasten her gown, but almost at once she heard the sound again. Whence did it come? Moving to the doorway, she rested her hand against the jamb, straining her ears. Then she gave a gasp and stared at her hand. A vibration was passing through the jamb from that distant, thunderous sound!

Snatching her hand away, she swung about and pressed both her palms against one wall and then another. The whole house was atremble! But it lasted only a matter of moments and then, apart from the creakings and groanings of settling boards and timbers, silence and stillness were restored. Badly frightened, she backed until she reached the edge of the bed, where she sat down slowly, terrified that the eerie vibrations would return. But five minutes passed and then half an hour. Had Kingsmill started to play tricks on her already? Never could she remember anything more terrifying than that feeling of the whole house being in the grip of some strange, supernatural force that was rocking it to its foundations.

When eventually she put her head on the pillow and fell asleep she was still in her clothes.

# Eight

IN THE EARLY-MORNING LIGHT Harriette explored the house afresh to see if she could find some explanation for that extraordinary experience of the night before. She was struck by a fact that had not really occurred to her before: Bryony Lodge was a very creaky house. There was not a board that did not squeak or a hinge that did not screech to some extent. Had Bryony Lodge known similar abuse in the past?

In the cellars she made a close inspection of the walls. Great cracks showed everywhere, some wide enough for her to slide her hand into them, but all were old wounds, dark with time, suggesting that the house had shifted on its foundations long ago. How long ago? Could it have been thirty-five to forty years ago when a violent attack on the house had sent William Hardware rushing from it, never to return? Or had it been the day when Charlotte had lost her footing when it had shivered and trembled, plunging her to her death?

She noticed that no wine bottles lay in the racks, and this was in keeping with Mr. Hardware's abstinence, for never once at Perbroke Square had she known him to ask for anything more than a sip of barley water or a swig of tea. Turning her back on the cellars, she returned to the kitchen, where the cleaning women had just arrived.

She had two disappointments during the day. The first was that red-headed Martha could not move in that day as Harriette had hoped, not wanting to spend another night on her own in the house.

"You said in two or three days, ma'am," Martha said uncomfortably, "and I can't leave me mother in the cottage on 'er own, 'er bein' an invalid and all. Me married sister is takin' 'er into their cottage over at Yapton, but it don't fit in for 'er to go there 'fore tomorrow at the earliest. I might manage to move in then."

Harriette nodded. There was nothing for it but to spend one more night alone in Bryony Lodge. Toward noon she went upstairs to Charlotte's bedroom, where the chest stood, hoping to find in it some clue to the evil that possessed the house. It had been tendrils of that evil that had reached out to touch William Hardware wherever he went, and it had not been its full power that she had confronted in the attic at Perbroke Square.

Perhaps she would find a letter or diary in the chest that would tell her more about this eerie old house and explain exactly why her late husband had left it in flight. She believed she had gathered the reasons together, but supposition was one thing and facts were another.

She closed the bedroom door to prevent any interruption and went to kneel down in front of the chest. Inserting the key, she found it turned easily, having been in use daily all the time Mr. Hardware had been at Perbroke Square and no doubt before that time too. It did make quite a rasping noise, but when she lifted the lid she realized that the chest was of Spanish origin, an ornate mechanism being set under the lid, similar to a box that her father had once owned.

But it was the contents that she was interested to discover. The first thing she lifted up was a heavy sword in a scabbard, which lay on a folded coat. Was the sword the reason why Mr. Hardware had thrown up the lid of the chest each night in order that he could face the effigies armed with a blade that could hack them to pieces if his tortured mind imagined attack? She decided she must be right, because the coat underneath had not been disturbed for a long time, and as she took it out she saw there were the crumbling holes that moths make in all the folds. It had once been a fine coat with the wide skirts and rows of buttons such as were fashionable around the time of King George's coronation. Had Mr. Hardware been attired in it at his wedding? Although well worn, it had obviously been treasured.

Next a flat rosewood box lay revealed to her, finely inlaid, and in it on a bed of silk lay some pieces of jewelry. They must have belonged to Charlotte, and among the rings, bracelets, eardrops, and necklaces was a miniature set in pearls. A plain, plump-faced woman with gentle eyes and soft mouth stared out with eyes of an exceptional china blue. This must be Charlotte, a simple-hearted, trusting woman if one was to judge by the features with their open innocence. She would have cradled William Hardware's unhappy head to her bosom and soothed his troubles away. It was a cruel trick of fate that they should have been parted through such a tragic accident.

Studying the miniature carefully, Harriette could only see a similarity to herself in Charlotte in the color of hair, for they both had the same dark gold locks. It must have been the sheen of her hair that Mr. Hardware had seen from his window in Perbroke Square that had caused him to think for the moment that she was like his Charlotte.

Turning to the rest of the chest's contents, Harriette found a leather drawstring bag which contained about eighty gold coins, and a chess set, a sewing box, and a few books that bore Charlotte's maiden name on the flyleaf. There was also a pistol, some shot, and a powder flask, a pair of spurs, a twist of paper containing waistcoat buttons, and sundry other small items, as well as riding boots and some shirts of coarse linen.

With care she replaced everything except the pistol, which she thought would be useful to have in case of emergency and a need to defend herself.

Taking her new-found weapon into her own room, she loaded it and thrust it out of sight under her pillows where she could reach it easily. Thus armed, she felt she could protect herself against any intruder.

The brightest time of the day was when Benedict arrived with the mare and gig, which delighted her. The animal was dappled gray with a mane and tail that hung like white silk.

"Now I can drive wherever I like," she declared proudly, the ribbons in one hand, a whip in the other, as she drove the gig out into the country lane, Benedict sitting beside her.

They drove as far as the seashore and he pointed out a ramp where fishermen's boats were drawn up. There was space enough for the gig, and down they went onto the golden, tide-rippled sands, which they followed for about three-quarters of a mile before turning up another ramp and regaining a country lane which led them through a small resort, where they stopped to take refreshment in a bow-fronted coffeehouse before returning to South Bersted. Harriette had purchased a bunch of cowslips from a Gypsy girl outside the coffee shop, and when they drew near the church she told Benedict, who had taken over the driving, that she wanted to visit Charlotte's tomb by daylight.

They alighted, and he looped the reins to a hitching post before following her into the churchyard. He found her in the cave of foliage created by the overhanging trees, and in the green-gold light she had placed the bunch of wildflowers on the flat surface of the tomb by Charlotte's name.

"There," she said, stepping back to look at the vivid yellow blooms lying on the dark stone. "That's better. I'll bring her some more flowers from time to time. Her resting place has been forgotten and neglected for too many years."

She was delighted when she returned to Bryony Lodge to find that the laundry woman had been there in her absence and rehung all the curtains and hangings, giving the house a more comfortable look.

"I'll be back at seven to take you to supper with Dr. Keane," Benedict said, having handed the mare over to James Willow to unharness and feed in the stable.

"It was hospitable of him to invite us," she said. "I'm to arrange which day he shall take me to Rowlands Castle."

It proved to be an enjoyable evening. Dr. Keane believed

in a good table and good company, and several of the guests were already known to Harriette from her meeting with them at Benedict's home. She began to feel she was settling down and becoming part of the community already.

Some of her high spirits deflated when the evening was over and she knew she faced another night alone in Bryony Lodge, but she hid her unease from Benedict, taking comfort from the knowledge that she had a pistol under her pillow, although what good that would be against a spectral presence or a shaking house she did not know, and some of the confidence she had had earlier in the day ebbed away. She had told Benedict about opening Mr. Hardware's chest, but not about the way the house had trembled, which had seemed too fantastic to relate, and she felt he must think her overimaginative already with her talk of ghosts and the near murder of Charlotte, for—like Dr. Keane—he was more inclined to accept it as an accident than to consider her version seriously.

Benedict stayed an hour with her before going back to Holly Wood House, and it seemed like a little reprieve not to be left on her own at once. There was also much comfort in his kisses and caresses, and for a while she put from her mind the emptiness of the house that was waiting to envelop her when he left again.

When at last he departed it was well past midnight, and she was thankful that the night had been shortened for her. Slowly she went up to her room, hating the way every stair creaked a dozen times over, setting the banisters astir, and then the rail, and on and on as though the echoes of every step went right through every stone and brick and tile of the house.

She was on the brink of sleep when an icy draft swept across her face like the brush of a hand. Sitting bolt upright in bed, her heart hammering, she stared fearfully around her. The moon had gone behind a cloud, but it was not too dark for her to pick out the furnishings of the room, and the door, which she had left ajar, was still in the same position. Yet the temperature of the room had fallen to icy depths, and again there came to her a whiff of that foul stench that had assailed her nostrils on her first day in the house. She clapped a hand over her nose, but she knew now what it was. Such a stench drifted on the wind from a body swinging in chains on a gibbet. Any last doubts in her mind as to the source of the evil in the house were swept away. It sprang from the restless soul of Thomas Kingsmill, which had sought out William Hardware to take revenge and was now directing it toward her!

She made no attempt to reach for the pistol. Such a weapon was useless. Courage was the only shield she could use for protection, and she must summon up every scrap of it in her trembling body. Slowly she turned back the covers of the bed and put her feet to the floor. The stench had gone again, but the chill remained in a draft that dragged, flicking her hair and the ribbons of her night shift toward the door.

She obeyed the silent summons of it, and the floorboards were like ice under her feet as she went out onto the landing. The draft was swirling away under the door that led to the servants' staircase, and with her throat parched with fear she turned her steps toward it. Some confrontation awaited her and it had to be faced sooner or later. Better this night before her nerves were worn down as William Hardware's had been.

Turning the handle, she went through and descended the dark flight. When she reached the kitchen she saw that the door to the courtyard stood open wide. Looking neither to the left nor to the right, she obeyed the tugging direction of her wildly dancing hair and went out through the door into the courtyard. There she paused, uncertain which way to go. The courtyard was flecked with silver and shadows as the scudding clouds allowed the moon to peep out and vanish again. Then she saw how the tall grass between the red bricks bent toward the orchard. Something awaited her there!

For a few moments she could not force herself to move, feeling half blind, half deaf with terror. But she had come this far and to retreat would be to condemn herself to endless persecution. She must go ahead! She must!

With her eyes fixed on the orchard beyond she began to make her way in a direct line across the courtyard, the waving grass and weeds brushing against the soft cambric of her night shift. One step after another she took, moving like a sleepwalker. Somewhere an owl hooted. On she went, direct as an arrow making for its target, never wavering, a pale figure in that odd, moon-shot setting.

"Harriette! Stop!" The roar of Benedict's voice came from the head of the flight of steps leading down from the stable loft.

She jerked to a halt, turning her stunned, white face toward him, bringing her shaking hands up to clasp them against her chest. He was hurling himself down the steps, and he leapt the last three and charged toward her. She gasped as he snatched her back with him and pointed down at a gaping black hole in the middle of the courtyard, on the edge of which she had been poised.

"For God's sake! You were making straight for the well!"

She stared at it in horror, unable to speak. Her mind seemed unable to function. She could not ask him why he was there, or how he knew the well lay in her path, or even how he had come to spring to her rescue in that last split second of time which had stood between her and death by drowning in the unspeakable horror of that slimy black well. Only one terrible fact stood out in her consciousness. Such a death had been meted out to the customs officer, William Galley, by the Hawkhurst gang in that terrible double murder that they committed on the Downs not all that many miles from where she now stood, clutching Benedict's coat lapels with frenzied hands, her eyes dilated and unblinking.

"K-K-K—" She tried to stammer Kingsmill's name, wanting to warn Benedict, but her teeth were chattering with shock and nothing coherent came from her.

Benedict put his warm palm gently and reassuringly over her mouth. "Don't talk, my darling. Not yet. Time enough for all you want to tell me when I have you safely indoors."

Effortlessly he picked her up and carried her through to the drawing room. There he laid her on a sofa, covered her with his own coat, and knelt to light the logs left ready in the fireplace. As soon as the blaze started to crackle he left her for a few minutes to go down to the cellar. To his surprise he found no bottles left there, and supposing that William Hardware had not been inclined to alcohol, he returned to the kitchen. There he filled a kettle with water, collected the tea caddy, a teapot, and cups, and went back to the drawing room.

"I'm going to make you some tea," he said, looking down at her before stooping to set the kettle on the fire. "I can't find any brandy in the cellar."

She still could not speak. When he took a seat on the edge of the sofa, looking down at her, she raised herself and put her arms about his neck, burying her face against his shoulder, and he held her shivering body close to him.

When the steam started to hiss from the kettle he made the tea and filled one of the cups with the pale, golden brew. He held it for her against her chattering teeth and she sipped it gratefully. She was more composed by the time she had finished it, and the second cup he poured for her she was able to hold for herself, propped against the cushions he had piled up behind her.

"Feeling better?" he asked.

She nodded, and still had some difficulty in speaking. "I—I didn't know—about—the well."

"I'm not surprised. It was completely hidden by the weeds surrounding it. There used to be a wooden lid covering it, but that has probably rotted to pieces and fallen in. I remember looking down into the well once when I was exploring the grounds years ago."

"Thank you—for—not going home."

"I didn't like the idea of your being alone in the house, so I sent the carriage back without me. I spent last night above the stables too, keeping watch in case that rogue Hammond took it into his head to return. I could hardly believe my eyes when I crossed to the loft window in time to see you making straight for the well, your gaze fixed far ahead. You weren't sleepwalking. Where were you going?"

"To the orchard. I—I thought it was there that the—the danger awaited me. Instead it lay under my feet."

"What danger?"

She looked down at the cup she held in her hands. "You told me once that you didn't believe in ghosts. But do you believe that some men are so evil that their wickedness can linger on to ruin the lives of those against whom they held a grudge?"

"I'd need proof," he admitted. "I'm a skeptic about such matters."

She considered carefully, draining the last sip of tea and putting the cup aside. "Perhaps if I tell you all that happened since I first heard Mr. Hardware's distressed shouts and sobbing through the wall at Perbroke Square, you will consider that you have proof enough."

"Tell me," he requested. "Let me judge the facts for myself."

She told him everything as she remembered it. The hands of the clock on the mantel moved on to half the hour of three o'clock by the time she concluded with an account of the strange manifestation that had drawn her out of Bryony Lodge and into such danger.

"So you see, I cannot believe that it was not some spectral design that I should end my days on this earth—not as poor Charlotte did with a fall down the stairs with its fatal consequences but in a manner similar to the terrible fate that overtook Galley and Chater. What happened tonight has convinced me on that point without a shadow of a doubt."

Benedict said nothing for a little while, thinking over all that she had said. His intelligent, logical mind weighed the facts and found them wanting. Drafts in old houses were often cold, and Benedict could find no significance in the one that had set the effigies whirling in the attic at Perbroke Square. But it had been a gruesome sight for a young and frightened girl who had had more than enough to cope with during the long months of nursing a cantankerous invalid, and he could see how it must have alarmed her. Then her first glimpse of Bryony Lodge had been a disappointment, not turning out to be the little cottage that she had hoped for. It had looked eerie enough in its dust and cobwebs, and the stench was explained away by dry rot or a dead rat under the floorboards or some other equally humdrum if slightly nauseating cause. No wonder Harriette associated it with the stench of death, for she must have seen a figure swinging on a wayside gibbet as often as he had, and when the wind blew in the wrong direction it could be deucedly unpleasant. Then there was the icy current of air, which she believed to have been some spectral manifestation, but which he knew had come from the open door that somehow or other had blown wide. The curve in the servants' stairway explained the odd distortion of the current's direction, and for Harriette in a highly nervous state it must have seemed as if the long-dead Thomas Kingsmill was calling her out to a rendezvous with death.

"You're not convinced," Harriette said quietly.

He turned toward her, knowing that she had read his thoughts. "I cannot lie to you. To me there is a perfectly simple and straightforward explanation for all that has happened. What is more, I think you must admit that William Hardware was more than a little mad. Harmlessly mad, but mad nevertheless."

"Do you think I'm mad too, then?" she questioned with a flash of her eyes.

"Indeed I do not!" he declared vehemently, "but you must guard against becoming obsessed by these extraordinary fears that old Hardware appears to have passed on to you."

"It's too late for warnings. I realize that, no matter what you say. Until my fears are conquered I'll be at the mercy of Kingsmill as Mr. Hardware was. Therefore I must find out what passed between them and I'm not going to wait until you are able to go to London, because it could be ages even then before the records come into your hands." There was a purposeful set to her face. "Dr. Keane has found out that the White Hart tavern at Rowlands Castle is still owned by the Paine family—and it was Mrs. Paine who betrayed Galley and Chater to the smugglers. Her son, Thomas, who was present when the two men were taken by the smugglers, lives there to this day, and I'm hoping he will be able to tell me something of William Hardware and whatever it was that Kingsmill threatened him with at the Newgate trial."

"I would prefer that you did not go to Rowlands Castle." Benedict looked grave. "Could you not give up delving into the past? It is preying on your mind."

She looked away from him. "Perhaps it is the only way to save my life—even my sanity."

He put his hand under her chin and turned her face back toward him. "Do you really believe that with Hardware's goods and properties you have inherited some curse that he lived under to the end of his days?"

Benedict had put it into words for her at last. Her eyes broke on the relief of sharing the burden with someone whom she could trust with all her heart.

"I do!"

"In that case all else shall be put aside until this matter has been settled once and for all. I cannot let you go on believing that you are being haunted in some way. You are right to want to find out everything you can about Hardware—the more we know the easier it should be to clear up the whole thing. I'll take you to the White Hart at Rowlands Castle tomorrow—"

She touched his hand. "Dr. Keane would be disappointed if I did not let him take me as arranged. I told him this evening that next Thursday would be convenient for me."

"Very well. In the meantime I'll investigate those cracks in the cellars and try to find out why the house vibrated in the extraordinary way you described to me."

She sat up with effort from the cushions. "Forgive me, Benedict, but I must go to bed. I feel so tired."

He helped her to her feet and took her face between his

hands, kissing her first on the forehead, the eyelids, and then gently on the mouth.

"Sleep well. I'll stay here by the fire. It is a great deal more comfortable than the stable loft, but I promise to be gone at first sight of the cleaning women coming up the drive. It would not do to start a scandal by my presence here."

He was pleased to see the corners of her lips curl into a suspicion of a smile. "How will you escape their eagle eyes?"

"I'll go out across the stableyard and climb the orchard wall. You forget I know my way around these grounds."

The smile showed again, sleepy and exhausted, and briefly she put her face against his in gratitude and—although she was not yet aware of it—the beginnings of love.

# Nine

Harriette drew up in her dainty blue-painted gig outside the church gates. Picking up a basket of flowers from the seat beside her, she alighted. After looping the mare's reins to a hitching post she entered the church gates.

She was feeling singularly happy, being much more at ease in her mind since she had confided everything to Benedict. What was more, she had had no more frightening experiences since the night when she had almost fallen down the well, and she was certain this was due to Benedict's presence in the house at night, for he had continued to return each evening after dark, even though James had moved into the stable loft and Martha into the servants' quarters under the eaves. The cleaning women had put the house completely in order and it shone with polish and scrubbed stone and woodwork. Now, with everything in order and Martha's company at night, she had told Benedict that he need no longer feel obliged to be her sentinel throughout the dark hours, and he had, somewhat reluctantly, agreed to leave Bryony Lodge to the watchful eye of James.

She held back the branches and went under them to Charlotte's tomb. Then she frowned. The bunch of cowslips which she had placed so carefully by Charlotte's name were limp and withered as she had expected, but the strange thing was that they lay in a little heap in the grass at the side of the tomb, almost as though they had been swept off the flat surface with a brush of the hand. The wind must have done it, she thought. But then surely they would have been scattered in a more haphazard way?

Out of the basket she took the flowers that she had picked in the garden of Bryony Lodge, as well as a vase to hold them, which she filled from a bottle of water brought for that purpose. Holding the vase in her hand, she looked for a suitable spot to put it and decided to place it at the foot of the tomb. Stooping down, she scraped away the leaves and twigs that had settled there, and pulled out some clumps of grass to make a little hollow in which to set securely the base of the vase. When it was in place she gave a final arrangement to the flowers and then stepped back as far as she could within that enclosed space to regard the result. Well pleased, she began to weed the ground surrounding the plinth of the tomb, and finally she took the garden shears, which she had brought in her basket, and clipped the grass to an even length, making it neat and tidy.

With the dead cowslips and rubbish in her basket she stood to approve the work she had done. Next time she would start removing the lichen from the stone or else soon the wording would be completely obliterated. The last thing she did before leaving was to make sure that the vase was well set into the ground and would not fall over.

The good weather continued and it was a glorious blue-gold day when Dr. Keane called for Harriette in his phaeton to take her to Rowlands Castle.

"Are we not fortunate with the weather, Mrs. Hardware?" the doctor said when she was settled in the seat beside him.

"We are indeed." She tilted her parasol against the sun. "I shall enjoy seeing the beauty of the Sussex countryside, but first I have something to confide to you."

"Yes?" Dr. Keane flicked the whip and the two horses moved forward. "I am at your service, ma'am."

"I have to tell you that my late husband, William Steele Hardware, was one of the two smugglers who gained a pardon through turning King's evidence."

The doctor showed no surprise. "Mr. Hardware said enough in his state of distress for me to gather that, but doctors and priests have the same code of honor, ma'am, when secrets are revealed. Had I needed confirmation of what I suspected, the name on his wife's tombstone would have settled it."

"Somebody else in the district knew the same secret."

"Harry Hammond, I don't doubt."

She gave him a sideways glance. "Is there nothing that you do not know, Dr. Keane?"

"In this village, not very much."

"Then do you know the identity of the present-day smugglers in the district? They are—according to Benedict—bringing in goods regularly for distribution further afield."

The doctor watched the lane ahead. "I am interested in crime and punishment, as I told you once, but I am not the law. I suspect, as Benedict suspects, and I keep my eyes open when I go on my rounds, but I tell you honestly that I have not a scrap of evidence that would hold up in court. Revenue men have raided the cellars and barns and byres in this district more times than anyone can remember, but not once has as much as a single keg of brandy or a pound of tea come to light. Wherever the goods are stored—as stored they must be at times when a boatload comes in—the hiding place has never been found."

"At least the local smugglers are not murderous—like the Hawkhurst gang."

"Do not underestimate them. I admit that the Hawkhurst crimes go unmatched, but some very unpleasant deeds are still committed in this apparently peaceful area. I have seen a number of drowned men who have—in my opinion—been silenced, and have not met their deaths accidentally. No proof though. Never any proof."

The phaeton continued to bowl along at a spanking pace. They drove by way of Chichester and on through Funtington, stopping at midday to take some refreshment at a coaching inn. Eventually, leaving Standsted Forest away on their right

162

hand, they came to Rowlands Castle, which she thought was a singularly ill-named village, there being no sign of a castle and—according to the doctor—nobody could remember if there had ever been one.

When the swinging sign of the White Hart came into sight Harriette thought pityingly of the two doomed men who had ridden along this same cobbled street all those years ago to stop for refreshment within its doors, thereby inadvertently condemning themselves to terrible deaths.

The doctor drew up in the tavern's courtyard and an ostler took the horses' bridles. Together Harriette and the doctor entered the White Hart and found themselves in a low-ceilinged taproom which smelled strongly of stale tobacco smoke, ale, and sawdust. A young lad was wiping the bar, and he dipped his head politely, pausing to dry his hands on his apron.

"Good day, sir—and madam."

"We wish to speak to Mr. Thomas Paine," the doctor said.

"'E ain't too well, sir. 'E's old, yer know."

"Nevertheless, I trust he will spare us half an hour. Please tell him that Dr. Keane of South Bersted and Mrs. Steele Hardware have come all this way specially to have a few words with him."

The lad gave them a curious look, but disappeared into a back room. When he returned he gave a nod. "Mr. Paine will see you. Come through 'ere, if you please."

In spite of the warmth of the day a fire was burning in the grate of the small parlor where an elderly man sat in a high-backed chair, his hands resting one over the other on a stick which stood propped between his wide-apart knees. He mumbled a reply to the doctor's greeting, and indicated with an upward sweep of his stick the two chairs that had been placed opposite him. But it was Harriette who held his attention, his gaze sharp and penetrating.

"Ye're Mrs. Steele Hardware, I'm told," Thomas Paine said in a rasping voice. "Why *Ardware* as well? That were the nickname we give Steele in the old days. Steele—'ardware. See the connection?"

"Then he was known only by that nickname for many years before I knew him," she said.

"Dropped 'is real name, did 'e? I ain't surprised. 'E 'ad good reason, I suppose." He frowned slightly. "'Ow come you 'ave 'is name anyway? What does it mean? Did William 'ave a son and ye be 'is granddaughter?"

"He had no son. I was his second wife."

Mr. Paine's eyes narrowed. "Went in for cradle snatching at the end, did 'e? Never would 'ave thought it of 'im."

"Har-um." The doctor coughed, hoping to remind the old man that he was addressing a lady. Such coarseness of expression was offensive to him, but there could be worse to come if he did not do something to avert it.

Mr. Paine threw him a mocking glance. "Got a nasty cough there, Doctor. Ain't you no physic to cure it?" With a cackle he turned back to Harriette. "You must 'ave a good reason for comin' to see me. Out with it."

"I want to ask you a question or two about the Hawk-hurst gang."

The old man's face gave nothing away, but his gnarled hands tightened on the head of his stick. "If I answered every dam'-fool question that's been put to me about the 'Awkhurst gang over the years I'd 'ave 'ad no time to eat or drink or sleep. I don't talk about it. To nobody."

"But you have received me! You must have realized it could only be something connected with the Hawkhurst gang that I would want to speak about."

"I were curious to know who it were that was coming with a name I ain't 'eard spoke in a long time."

Harriette leaned forward in her chair. "Please believe I would not have come troubling you unless it was important —and it is of vital importance to me to gather a certain piece of information. You were acquainted with my late husband. You can tell me things about his early years that nobody else knows."

Thomas held up his hand to indicate the need to clarify matters. "Ye must remember that I were a lad—full-grown, but still a lad—to William's twenty-odd years when 'e used to come and go for 'is pint of ale in this tavern, and 'e never as much as passed the time of day with me. So don't go thinking I can give ye 'is life's 'istory up to that time, 'cos I can't. But tell me what it is ye want to know, and mebbe I can 'elp ye and mebbe I can't."

Encouraged, she drew in her breath. "I have been given a brief account of the murder of Chater and Galley, and I know that my late husband turned King's evidence—"

"Aye! 'E betrayed 'is old comrades right enough and gained a free pardon for it," Thomas sneered, "even though 'e were with Cobby and 'Ammond and Carter and rest of 'em when they whipped Galley to death and put 'im down the well at Lady Holt Park and buried Chater alive!"

Harriette shuddered and drew back in her chair, clutching the arms of it. "It is the leader of the Hawkhurst gang, Thomas Kingsmill, that I want to know about. He threatened the witnesses at his trial. Did he issue any special threat against my late husband?"

"Threat? It were a curse!"

"What was it, Mr. Paine?"

"He swore to 'ound William to 'is grave and 'is kin after 'im!"

Harriette went white to the lips, and Dr. Keane, fearing she might faint, half rose in his chair, but she shook her head to reassure him that she was all right. "That is what I thought it might be, Mr. Paine," she said in a level voice.

"Were you present at the Newgate trial, Mr. Paine?" the doctor inquired.

"No, but I talked to them who was. Glover told me all about it. 'E was taken with Kingsmill and Fairall and Perrin, but 'e were acquitted, and 'e were that thankful to get let off that 'e turned religious. Never missed a Sunday in church after that till the day 'e died." Thomas cocked his head at Harriette. "What about William? Did 'e end 'is days in sackcloth and ashes?"

"In a way he did," Harriette answered quietly.

"I ain't surprised to 'ear it. 'E were the first to suggest throwing Galley and Chater down a well. Mind ye, 'e were sitting out in that taproom"—here he jerked a thumb over his shoulder in the direction of the door—"and 'ad more than a few mugs of ale inside 'im. I know, 'cos I were pulling pints that day. 'E were full of bravado—showing off, ye might say—and knowing all the time that Galley and Chater were drunk and harmless in an upstairs room and likely only to be shipped off to France on a smuggling schooner and kept out of the way somewhere." The contemptuous sneer returned to Thomas's face and he wagged a bony finger at Harriette, one eye half closed. "Let me tell ye there were no one more worried than 'e was when Galley and Chater were brought downstairs with blood all over their faces and carried out to be tied together on one of the 'orses—which 'e 'ad the job of leading over the Downs. When the whipping of the two prisoners started, William kept shouting out to the other smugglers to stop it, 'cos 'e kept getting the ends of the lashes across 'is shoulders. But after that 'e did nothing to save either Galley or Chater—and ye know the finish of the story."

"I believe you held the horse while these two unfortunate men were tied onto it together," the doctor said, his eager inquisitiveness overcoming his tact.

Thomas glowered dangerously. "I only brought that 'orse into the White Hart's courtyard and 'eld it for a few minutes. I 'ad no part in the murders. What 'appened 'ad nothing to do with me. My 'ands are clean."

"But it was your mother who sent word to the smugglers that Galley and Chater were here taking refreshments under her roof," the doctor persisted, not heeding the ominous signs of Thomas's growing agitation, "and I feel bound to point out that if she had not abused the age-old unwritten laws of hospitality the murders would never have taken place."

"Get out!" Thomas waved his stick furiously, his countenance turning purple. "I'll talk no more to either of ye! Get out! Get out, the pair of ye—and never come back again!"

"We had better go, Mrs. Hardware," the doctor said quickly, but Harriette had already risen to her feet.

"Goodbye, Mr. Paine," she said with dignity, and turned toward the door.

When the doctor left her at the door of Bryony Lodge, Harriette entered slowly and with reluctance. What she had heard from Thomas Paine had only confirmed what she had already guessed, but the whole interview had unnerved her more than she had realized and it was with dread and hatred that she looked around the hall of the house that was hers.

"You are home in good time, Mrs. Hardware." It was Martha who had come from the kitchen quarters, neat and smiling in her blue cotton dress and white apron, her round, freckled face framed by her cap. "Was it not a pretty ride?"

"Very pretty indeed." Harriette untied her bonnet and removed it. "I trust Cook has not forgotten that Mr. Sutcliffe is coming to supper."

"No, madam. She has prepared a cold collation as you wished."

Harriette went up the stairs to her room. Creak, creak, creak. Was it her imagination, or was every board in the house looser than before? Benedict had been puzzled by the cracks in the cellar walls, concluding as she had done that years and years ago some land subsidence had caused the house to resettle on its foundations, but he had found nothing to explain the odd vibration of the walls that she had told him about.

There was time for a walk before Benedict arrived. She welcomed the thought after the long drive that day. Changing her coat for a cloak, she sped down the stairs again and out into the evening air. She walked briskly, finding balm for her anxieties in the soft air. When she came within sight of the sea she sat on a gate and watched the sky change color as the red ball of the sun set behind the black trees.

The path she took back to the lane brought her close to the churchyard, where a gate offered a shortcut. Almost of their own volition her steps took her to the corner where Charlotte lay, her thoughts being wrapped up in all she had heard at the White Hart. Then she gave a gasp of mingled annoyance and dismay. The vase of flowers, which she had arranged with such care, lay on its side, the flowers crushed by a careless foot that had pressed them into the earth. Who could have come to this quiet corner and wreaked the damage? And less than ten minutes ago to judge by the pool of water which had not yet soaked away.

She straightened the vase and put the flowers to rights as best she could. But she gave the tomb a backward glance before she left. Surely it had not been a deliberate act of vandalism that had swept aside a simple gesture of remembrance to a woman who had never done anyone any harm?

Benedict on horseback overtook her at the gate of Bryony Lodge. He dismounted at once and a gladness at seeing him swept through her so strongly that it lit up her face and he was encouraged to put an arm about her as they walked together up the drive, and it was not rejected.

After supper they were alone in the house. The cook and the scullery maid came in daily from the village and departed when the supper dishes were done, and Martha spent her spare time with James. Benedict had heard all that had taken place at the White Hart, and inwardly he was more than a little angry that there should have been talk of a curse to disturb and upset Harriette even more.

"It's a great pity we cannot know William Hardware's exact reaction to Kingsmill's words," Benedict said. "After all, he was only a young man at the time. I cannot believe he would not have shrugged it off—unless, of course, his mind was already unbalanced by extreme qualms of conscience. From what Thomas Paine said to you it does seem as though Hardware felt a personal responsibility for the murders by being the first to suggest—however wildly—that those two innocent men be thrown down a well."

"I had hoped to find something written down in his sea chest. But I found nothing."

Benedict's face tightened with interest. "His sea chest! That's the one you told me about. Are you sure there was nothing in it? Did you look for a concealed panel or a secret compartment?"

"No, I didn't. Perhaps there is something there that I didn't discover!" She sprang to her feet. "Let's go and look!"

Benedict knelt with her when she unlocked the chest and lifted the lid. Together they removed the contents, and he examined each box and container to make sure that nothing was tucked away inside. Finally he tapped and prodded every side and corner of the chest, tipping it on its side to make sure that it did not have a false bottom, and in the end he rose up from the floor with a sigh.

"Nothing! You don't suppose you overlooked anything in the house at Perbroke Square, do you?"

She was replacing everything with care. "I'm certain that anything of importance would be in this chest. It was the only thing he had that contained any personal possessions." She had reached the coat, and she sat back on her heels, unfolding it for the first time. "I think I should throw this away. There are moths in it." Then as her hand ran over the pocket something crackled inside it. She and Benedict exchanged a surprised glance, suddenly alert. He dropped down to one knee beside her and she dived her hand into the pocket and drew out a sheaf of papers that were covered with closely written handwriting. Together their heads bent over it, and they saw at once that the heading was that of Bryony Lodge, South Bersted.

"Mr. Hardware wrote it while he was still living here!" Harriette exclaimed.

"*This is my true confession*," Benedict read aloud, "*written down in the hope that God will show mercy to a sinner who does repent wholeheartedly of years spent in folly and dissipation and crime, which led to murder most foul.*" He raised his head and looked at Harriette. "Is it your wish that I should read it privately, or are you sufficiently at ease with me to feel no embarrassment at whatever might come to light?"

She was touched by his courteous consideration, but he was the one person with whom she felt false modesty would be slightly ridiculous. "I must know what has been written down. Let us go downstairs, and you can read it to me where the light is better."

In the drawing room there in Bryony Lodge, Harriette at last came to know the man to whom she had been wife in name only. Without doubt drink and greed had been the downfall of that young man, William Steele Hardware, trained in an honest trade by respectable parents, but who had fallen into bad company, which had led to smuggling activities on an audacious scale. Never a leader, always needing the stimulation of alcohol to boost his courage, he had shown weakness and cowardice in failing to condemn the brutality of his fellow smugglers in their treatment of Galley and Chater. With complete frankness he wrote in detail of that terrible ride of death for the two poor victims from the Sunday afternoon to the night of the following Wednesday into Thursday. At each stop he had become drunk with the rest of the smugglers and, reeling helplessly, he had watched without any attempt to intervene when poor Chater had been cut about the eyes and nose while on his knees, begging for mercy. When the wretched fellow was eventually tossed down a well, William helped to thrust him over the pales, and although he had not cast stones at the victim when groans had announced that life still lingered, it was only through being incapacitated by violent sickness that William had dropped the rock in his hand.

"*Even though I did regret my evil deeds in the cold light of day and with a sober head,*" Benedict read on, "*it is to my everlasting shame that I made no attempt to contact the law until my name was given to the authorities in an anonymous letter, which could have come from any one of those I had abused in my time. Then I did turn King's evidence and had the added shame of suffering the scorn of my former colleagues after I had betrayed them.*" There followed a description of the trial, and then, some months later, hearing word of the whereabouts of Kingsmill, the Hawkhurst leader, William had denounced him to the authorities, and again was a witness. "*But before all those present Kingsmill did curse me, saying that he would not rest until he had hounded me to my grave, and all who were kin to me. How dreadfully has that curse pursued me, enforced as it was by the hatred of my former comrades whom I sent to the gallows. I have ever since felt that hatred dogging me, but it is Kingsmill himself who is ever nearby. I tried to escape him. When no longer young I met my sweet Charlotte, and for her sake I tried to take up again the way of life that my good parents instilled in me, forswearing hard drinking for evermore. Her father gave her this house and a sizable dowry, and we expected to live in comfort until the end of our days. But by a cruel trick of fate the son of one of my old comrades lived in the village, and from the day he first called on me I knew no peace from his blackmailing demands, because at all costs I wanted to keep my dreadful crimes from Charlotte's knowledge. I paid and paid, drawing on Charlotte's dowry when my own money was gone, but this was only part of my troubles. Kingsmill's evil was in the house, and such nightmares came to me that I shouted out many times before Charlotte did rouse me from my torment and hold me weeping in her arms. In that way did she discover my past, and begged me to make my peace with God. I had not set foot in God's house since first straying from an honest path, and with such a crime on my conscience I had never dared step on holy ground. It was a gray day with lashing rain when I rode off to say my prayers and beg for forgiveness, but when I reached the church gates I did see Kingsmill come down the path toward me with a keg on his shoulder and his hat over his eyes as in days gone by. Such terror seized me that my speech went from me and the pain in my chest cast me down into darkness. A passer-by found me staggering out of the gate and took me home in a cart. I did not tell Charlotte what I had seen, but I think she knew, for I would not set foot outside the house in the days that followed, and kept my sword at my side. Then Kingsmill took his true revenge, appearing to my Charlotte, who did scream and fall down the stairs. She gave birth to a premature infant daughter before she died, and then our sweet offspring did follow her to the grave. Now I am alone with Kingsmill, who seeks to drive me insane. Should I be found dead in Bryony Lodge, let all know that I beg that prayers for my soul be said by any who can find it in their hearts to pity a repentant sinner. Signed by my hand this thirteenth day of September in the year of our Lord 1773. William Steele Hardware."*

Benedict finished reading and he lowered the paper in his hand. He saw how tense and pale Harriette looked, and she released a sigh. "Well, he did not die in Bryony Lodge," she said slowly. "After another fright he rushed from it, and began his endless moving from house to house until eventually he settled in Perbroke Square. No wonder he consistently refused to see you, Benedict. He thought you intended to force him to return to Bryony Lodge over the matter of Hammond's neglect of the tenants, and he never wanted to set foot in it again."

"Suppose," Benedict said thoughtfully, "it was not a ghost he thought he saw in the churchyard, but by sheer chance he had happened on a local smuggler going about his business. There has always been a path across the fields and meadows between South Bersted and the sea, and in those days—before the wall was built—the churchyard would have provided a handy shortcut."

"I can accept that, and it also explains Mr. Hardware's collapse in Perbroke Square, having already suffered some severe damage to his heart, but it does not explain Charlotte's sight of Kingsmill. I cannot believe that she did not see his ghost in this house."

"Unless it was someone playing tricks? Hammond, perhaps. Obviously Hardware was becoming more and more reluctant to part with his wife's money, and Hammond, knowing about Kingsmill's curse, decided to frighten Hardware into parting with the money, but the plan went wrong and Charlotte was the victim."

She shook her head. "No. It didn't happen like that. Charlotte saw Kingsmill, I'm certain of it."

He moved closer to her on the sofa where they were sitting. "Then if you believe so strongly in the curse of Kingsmill you must end it here and now. I'm asking you to marry me, Harriette. To rid yourself of a surname that has brought you nothing but unhappiness. I love you. I've loved you since the moment I first saw you. Say you'll marry me."

She leaned forward and put her cheek against his, her eyes closed, her arms folding about his neck. He was dearer to her than anyone she had ever known, and perhaps when the ghost of Kingsmill had been laid she would be free to return that love a thousandfold, but she could not take the way out that he had offered her. It would solve nothing.

"Not yet, Benedict," she whispered, turning her lips to his.

He knew her words were a promise that her love was to come and he seized her in a passionate embrace, his kisses seeking the very heart of her.

# Ten

It was a wild and blowy afternoon. Harriette held tight to her billowing cloak as she followed one of her favorite paths to come within sight of the sea. There it lay, dark gray and turbulent, running with sinister-looking whitecaps in an exceptionally high tide. Enormous waves, thundering against the shore, threw up huge cascades of spray twenty feet high or more. It was an awesome sight and the thunder of the water blended with the distant thunder of a gathering storm. Even at a considerable distance from the water her face became dewed by spray carried in the wind, which laid a pearly mist over her cloak and hood.

She turned for home again by way of the path that took her close to the churchyard, and she decided to spend an hour scraping more lichen from Charlotte's tomb. The trees would give her some shelter from the wind and she found the work tranquil and relaxing.

Reaching Charlotte's secluded corner, she found the spot where she had secreted the tools she had been using for the scraping and decided to make a start on the sides, having already cleaned the east end of it. The lid she was leaving until last. Kneeling on the steps of the plinth, she commenced her work.

She sang softly to herself. Suddenly she paused, looking at the edge of the lid of the tomb. That was strange. There was no lichen along the edge of it, and it was smooth and worn as though it had been much handled.

She stared at it and crowding back into her mind came the memory of the cowslips that had fallen to the ground in a lump, the upset vase and the crushed flowers, and that brief line written by William Hardware about seeing Kingsmill come through the churchyard. Had Benedict been right in persuading her that it had been a very much alive smuggler going about his nefarious business? And had that smuggler been coming from some hiding place that was still being used for smuggled goods before their distribution? She knew that pulpits and vestries and vaults had been used for storage, because reports reached the newspapers of uncovered contraband, so why not a tomb too? A lifted lid would have sent the cowslips slipping off in the way they had!

Hardly daring to breathe, she put the palms of her hands under the lid and pushed. It lifted easily. On great hinges. Not knowing what she would see, Harriette leaned over and looked into the tomb. Her eyes widened. Instead of some boxes and kegs put on or alongside a coffin, as she had expected, there was a hole as dark as a well with an iron-runged ladder going down into it! Of a coffin there was no sign.

She closed the lid at once and leaned on it, breathing deeply. This was something she must not investigate alone. Benedict must be fetched at once!

She ran the short distance to Holly Wood House. Benedict, sighting her from his study window, threw open the front door and rushed out to meet her, having seen from her face that something was amiss.

"Charlotte's tomb! In the churchyard! It's empty! I lifted the lid! There's a ladder in it!"

"What are you saying?" he demanded in amazement.

"The smugglers must be using a cave or hole or an old, dry well beneath the tombs to store contraband!"

He drew her indoors to his study, sat her down, and questioned her. Then he paced thoughtfully up and down, holding his chin between finger and thumb, his brows meeting in a deep frown.

"You're quite sure nobody saw you open the tomb?"

"I'm positive."

"You didn't meet anyone in the churchyard or in the lane?"

"No one. It's such a blustery day that nobody is abroad unless they have to be."

"Then luck is with us." He went to his desk and sat down, drawing a sheet of paper toward him. Quickly he wrote and sealed it. "I'm sending to Chichester for the revenue men to come at once, but they are to muster here in the grounds of Holly Wood House after dark. I intend to catch those smugglers red-handed if the revenue men have to hide around the churchyard every night for a month or a year! In the meantime, after I've dispatched a fast rider with this letter, I'm going down into the tomb to have a look around for myself."

"No!" She leapt to her feet. "Suppose the smugglers should return and discover you!"

"They don't usually move around until after nightfall."

"But they have been there during the day. I know by the way a vase of flowers I'd put by the tomb in the morning was knocked over by evening."

He took her by the shoulders. "Then will you keep watch for me? You can kneel by another grave in full view of the lane and let me know by a signal if anyone comes anywhere in sight."

"I'll do that! I'd do anything for you, Benedict!"

They returned to the churchyard when he had seen his servant into the saddle and off at a gallop. Benedict had armed himself with pistols and had brought a lantern. He whistled with astonishment when he lifted the lid of Charlotte's tomb and looked at the black depths below.

"Don't stay here," he whispered to Harriette. "Go to the spot where you can keep a lookout."

She watched him climb down and he looked up and gave her a smile in the tiny glow of the lantern he held before he disappeared from her sight. Nervously she went and kneeled down by the grave of a Bersted man whose name meant nothing to her, and clipped away at the grass. A cart passed along the lane and some children ran by, shouting out how some of the fields were being flooded by the high tide, and once she saw two women hurrying home with baskets on their arms. But all had their heads down against the wind and the first heavy spots of rain that had started to fall, and not one as much as glanced toward the churchyard.

An hour had gone by when she heard a step in the other direction. She looked up and saw Benedict hastening toward her. By this time she was almost soaked to the skin by the rain, and drops of it showered off her cloak as she ran to him.

"Come on! Let's get back to Holly Wood House! I've much to tell you!" he said urgently.

In the study he described what he had seen. "A naturally formed subterranean passageway lies under the churchyard and reaches to the sea. I followed it for a considerable distance until I could tell by the noise that the sea had entered it. I suppose the tunnel comes out somewhere near the beach and it has been used for years—probably since the time of the Hawkhurst gang—for bringing in boatloads of smuggled goods in complete seclusion. I then turned back, passed the ladder again, and found the north-facing passageway blocked by a locked door. I tried forcing it, but it was impossible. Behind it must lie the contraband, and it's my belief that the smugglers will move to fetch it out tonight!"

"Why are you so sure?"

"Because of this very high tide! The water is sweeping in! Whatever goods lie behind that door will have to be moved as soon as it is dark, because the tide is by no means at its height yet!"

It seemed a long time to wait until the servant returned with the revenue officer, but actually the mission had been accomplished at a record pace. Benedict went out into the pelting rain to meet the officer and heard that he had wisely kept his troops waiting some short distance away in order that word of their arrival should not run through the village and alert the smugglers.

The revenue officer, whose name was Captain Crowhurst, congratulated Harriette on her part in discovering the hiding place which had eluded everyone else for so long.

"I'll send you back to Bryony Lodge in a carriage now,

Harriette," Benedict said. "It could be dangerous here near the church if there is a running battle."

She looked at him in dismay. "I want to be near you!"

"But you would have to stay indoors anyway. I'd feel more at ease to have you well out of range. In any case, there's an added danger that you'll go down with a fever if you don't get out of those rain-soaked clothes."

She certainly had a bedraggled appearance and her petti-coats were wet and clammy about her legs. "Very well. I'll go home and change into some dry things."

He did not see the rebellious glint in her eye. She intended to return in her dry clothes with her own pistol in her hand. Nobody—not even Benedict—was going to banish her from the scene of excitement.

"Take care!" she urged at the moment of leaving him. Then, fearful for his safety, she flung her arms about his neck and kissed him with a fierce sweet surge of passion. With a long, loving look at him over her shoulder she darted out to the carriage to climb in and be borne away.

The night was already pitch-black, except when a shaft of lightning turned the whole countryside a steely blue. Over-head the thunder rolled and rumbled and the rain slashed against the carriage windows. She thought there never could have been a more dismal night for the revenue men—and Benedict—to wait in hiding to capture smugglers.

The carriage departed and she let herself into the house. As soon as she had changed she intended to take her mare and gig and drive back to Holly Wood House again.

"Martha!" she called out. The house was in darkness. Not a single candle had been lit.

A flash of lightning enabled her to find the tinderbox in the hall and she lighted the candles in a branched candela-brum. She called out to her maid again, thinking her voice must have been drowned in the thunder, but Martha did not appear.

Harriette hurried along and pushed the door open to the kitchen, but apart from the glow in the range it was as dark as the rest of the house. It looked as if Martha and James had prolonged their outing somewhere.

How cold it was in the house! Her wet clothes added to her discomfort. The sooner she was out of them the better. But she must have more light. The shadows frightened her.

She knew where Martha kept the long taper holder, and the little flame streamed from it when she lighted the chandelier in the hall and went from sconce to sconce along the walls, creating an ever-increasing and comforting glow of candlelight.

She had put the taper away again and was crossing the hall toward the staircase when there was such a plummeting in temperature that she caught her breath at the freezing atmosphere. Coming to a halt, she looked warily about her, her hand holding the candelabrum beginning to shake. The house was oddly silent and still as though it had given up trying to compete with the noise of the storm outside. For once its creakings were lost in the buffeting of the wind against the windows and in the crack of roll after roll of thunder above its roof.

Then there came a sound that she had never heard before. It was a faint swish-swish as though the hem of a cloak was being brushed across the floor of the room above, to and fro as though the wearer was not moving, but casting the cloak backward and forward on his arm.

She could not move. Who was it upstairs? Who was it that lurked there, waiting to meet her face to face when she reached the head of the stairs! The swishing was getting louder. Not like a cloak any longer, like the bristles of a broom going over the same spot. She wanted to cry out, but terror had her by the throat.

Suddenly something pattered onto the floor at her feet. Tiny fragments the color of pearls. Candle wax! She raised her head and looked upward at the high ceiling of the hall. Then she saw what had been causing that inexplicable, unfamiliar sound. Directly above her head the chandelier was swinging wildly to and fro, and long cracks were darting across the plasterwork. She stared at it as though hypnotized. There was no draft to swing it. Whatever was causing such an extraordinary pendulum movement? To and fro. To and fro. So wide was the swing that it was hitting the ceiling each time now and the light from the branched candelabrum that she held in her hand threw it into grotesque shadows which looked for all the world like an evil, grinning face.

Then her horrified eyes saw an enormous piece of plaster peel away from the ceiling and with it the whole chandelier. Life surged back into her numbed limbs. She hurled herself onto the stairs and saw it descend to crash to pieces within inches of her. In fact, so close was she that one of the ornate branches of the chandelier gagged the flow of her skirt when it came thumping and bumping to rest on the stair by her foot. It had ripped the material like the blade of a razor-sharp knife.

Somehow or other she willed herself not to give way to flight, and with a supreme effort she found her voice. "Kingsmill!" she croaked. "Be gone from this place!"

The effect of her words was like a spark to a fuse. All about her the house began to rumble as though some new kind of thunder had entered into the very bricks and mortar, threatening to bring the whole place tumbling about her ears. With a violent crack the pier glass on the wall opposite her disintegrated into glittering fragments, which were hurled about the floor. Another was smashed, and then another, as though thumped by an outraged fist in passing. Under her feet the stairboards trembled, and her horrified eyes saw the banister rail sway like a snake.

Screaming, she bolted up the stairway. The leaping light of the candelabrum in her hand threw terrifying shadows all about her, and she screamed again when she reached the landing, her dilated eyes seeing a tall chest toppling toward her. She swerved in time, but a heavy chair was flung across her path, causing her to fall headlong over it. The candelabrum flew from her hand, and she struck her head on the bottom step of the attic flight, the door to it standing open.

Stunned into immobility by the searing pain in her head, she lay full-length, hearing, but not seeing, the upturning of other furniture, the smashing of vases tilted from shelves, the splitting of ceiling plaster which descended in heavy flakes.

She smelled the smoke, but in her dazed state associated it with bonfires and London chimneys and the mean coals in the attic fireplace at Perbroke Square. Perhaps that was where she was. Lying for some unknown reason with her cheek on the cold polished boards, a limp arm over her face, while the smoke billowed and rolled over her. Yet in Perbroke Square there had been no maid called Martha. Why had she thought there was? The housemaids were called Annie and Rose and Nell and Meg. There were other servants too. And two little girls and their parents. Whatever were their names? Who else was it she was trying to remember? Someone whom she thought she had loved. But she loved no one but Benedict. She could recall distinctly the very first time she ever saw him. Once again she was looking directly into his open carriage window, out of which he stared at her with those bold, dark eyes that had sent an erotic spasm of excitement leaping through her. But he was driving away. Out of sight. She was alone in the black smoke that had started to seep under her protecting arm and was causing a cough in her throat. Then it came back to her where she was, and with great effort she lifted her head and saw the flames. The whole of the staircase was ablaze, ignited by the fallen chandelier, and the fire was spreading rapidly, making her aware that she must have been lying at the foot of the attic stairs much longer than she had realized. The way down the rear flight to the kitchen was still open, but she must not run from the house. This was the confrontation with Kingsmill that she had been dreading and expecting, and if she ran before him he would dog her to her grave, even as William Steele had been condemned to endless misery.

She coughed as she dragged herself to her knees, and she ripped with weak and shaking hands a piece from her torn skirt, which she dabbled in water that had trickled out from a fallen flower vase. Holding it over her mouth and nose, she crawled laboriously, often crumpling up and sprawling out on the floor again, toward the wall farthest away from the roaring staircase. She felt no amazement at failing to feel the scorching heat, knowing that Kingsmill's eerie presence hung icily around her, but she was weeping copiously, aware that she was as near the brink of hysteria as she would ever be, but she would not give way.

Reaching the paneled wall at last, she clutched at the jamb of the door that led into Charlotte's bedroom, and slowly she heaved herself up to her feet, terrified that her swimming head would whirl her into unconsciousness and then all would be lost, whether she lived or died. Twisting her body around, she managed to lean her back against the wall, trying not to let her sagging knees give way again. Mercifully a slight draft from the direction of the attic, although increasing the force of the flames, was at least blowing the smoke away from the particular spot where she was half standing, half lolling, and she lowered the soaked cloth from her face in order to speak out the better.

"I defy you, Kingsmill!" she uttered on a rising shout that rasped as her voice gathered strength, the note of determination unweakened by the crack and hoarseness of her smoke-affected throat. "I alone of all those you held in terror will not run from you! I'm young and alive and my will is stronger than yours!"

A beam, weakened by creeping flames, creaked, split away from its supports, and bounced down across the landing, completely cutting off the kitchen flight. She did not give it as much as a glance, keeping her gaze ahead, as though she could see Kingsmill in the darkness beyond the leaping flames. So high-pitched with tension was she that an intoxicating sense of triumph was beginning to course through her veins. She was no longer afraid. Fear was a transient thing and it existed for her no more. No matter what happened she was free of it. And the curse was at an end because of this blissful liberation!

She lurched away from the wall to stand swaying, arms

outflung at her sides, and she heard herself laughing. "It's all over, Kingsmill! This is your funeral pyre! Long-delayed, but no less purifying for that! The air is clean again! Your shadow has gone forever!"

Behind her the door to the servants' stairway was thrown open, causing a draft, which sent the flames leaping toward her, but Benedict snatched her to him and dragged her down the smoke-darkened flight. Several men who had accompanied him to help with the rescue clattered down ahead of them and streamed out into the stable yard, waving their arms to clear a path through their comrades gathered there.

Even as she appeared in the doorway with Benedict all the strength seemed to go from her limbs, and she reeled against him, coughing and half fainting. As he snatched her up in his arms a warning shout came from one of the revenue men, who was holding a captured smuggler by a rope.

"Look out! The roof's collapsing!"

Benedict sprang forward with Harriette, racing away from the tremendous roar of tumbling masonry that was making the cobblestones of the yard shake and writhe beneath his feet. Past the well he went, willing hands helping him on his way, and he reached the safety of the orchard in time to turn with her clutched tight to him and see Bryony Lodge collapse like a pack of cards, throwing out smoke and flame and a mad fireworks display of sprouting red-gold sparks.

He knew what had happened. The subterranean passageways, honeycombing the earth beneath the house, had caved in, destroyed by the flooding sea water that was surging inland on the crest of the mighty tide. Watching, he and the others saw an enormous indentation appear across the stable yard from the well to the house, showing that yet another tunnel was crumbling in fall after fall of earth below the surface.

The captured smuggler gave a despairing groan. He had been first out of the tomb in the churchyard, a sack of tea on his shoulder, but his sharp eyes had spotted the glint of a musket in the foliage and his warning shout had given Hammond and the other smugglers time to double back again behind the underground door, barricade it, and avoid capture.

"They're trapped!" he moaned, gaunt-faced. He had been given a choice by Captain Crowhurst of a blade between the ribs or to divulge where the smugglers would emerge from the ground in an escape route. He had told them there was a way out in the wall of the well in the stable yard of Bryony Lodge, certain that they would branch away under the house and come up near Hammond's farm, but now his comrades were all lost anyway, crushed beneath earth and root and stone.

Benedict laid Harriette gently on the grass and knelt beside her. To his relief he saw that she appeared to have suffered no ill effects from the fire, although there was a cut on her forehead and a livid bruise on her cheek. She opened her eyes and there was a look of serenity on her face.

"You're safe now," he said, holding her hand between his.

A faint smile showed on her lips and she nodded, knowing that all was well at last.


Not until Harriette was fully recovered from her ordeal did Benedict tell her what had been found in the stable.

"The coffin containing Charlotte and her baby had been removed there by Hammond and the other smugglers many years ago," he said. He was sitting with her on a white-painted garden seat under a shady tree in the walled garden of Holly Wood House, and when he saw the start of distress in her eyes he was quick to reassure her. "It was unharmed. It had been walled up in an aperture, and if some of the bricks had not fallen away when part of the building collapsed with the house it would never have been found." A frown creased his brow. "Yet I should have suspected that something was hidden there. I ought to have known. It was years since I'd clambered around in those grounds as a boy, but on that first morning I was there after you had moved in I knew that there was something different about the building, and yet what it

*184*

was escaped me. It was simply that a small window had been bricked up."

She looked down at the rose in her hand, which he had picked for her when they had come out into the morning sunshine. "Has she been—reinterred?"

"Yes, my dearest. That has been done."

"Why had her tomb been singled out to be used as a way in and out of the tunnels?"

"Hammond explained all that at his interrogation after he and a few others managed to crawl back to the tomb and face the men we left battering in the underground door there. He had realized that when Hardware left the village without warning he would not be back. The tomb was in a sheltered spot, and there were wooded routes over the low wall that enabled them to come and go without being seen. In addition there was nobody in the village close enough to either William or his wife who would ever go to the tomb."

"Then you were right in thinking that Mr. Hardware saw a live smuggler on the day he went to the churchyard. What will happen to Hammond and the other smugglers who were rescued?"

"They are to be tried at Chichester, but it depends on the judge whether they face hanging or transportation."

"Have all the other bodies been recovered?"

"Yes. None lies beneath the ruins of Bryony Lodge. The smugglers were branching off along another route which would have brought them up near Hammond's farmhouse, but once the earth falls started there was no stopping the chain reaction that resulted. It is no wonder the revenue men never found any contraband in the past. They looked for more conventional hiding places, never realizing that everything was literally under their feet."

"That strange vibration that affected the house the first night I was in it on my own. What was the cause of that?"

"The smugglers were rolling in a shipment of brandy kegs. They never realized how unsafe the house had become."

"How frightened I was," she said reminiscently.

"Bryony Lodge and all its terrors for you have gone forever. Even the subterranean passageways have been filled in through the action of the sea. The land is whole again."

She sat silent for a little while. Nothing would shake her conviction that she had confronted Kingsmill that night, no matter how or why the destruction of the house had been brought about. But as Benedict said, that was all behind her now.

"I should like the rubble of Bryony Lodge cleared away," she said, her decision made, "and no trace of it to remain. Let the land be used to build cottages to rehouse the unfortunate people in those hovels. Does that sound a good proposition to you?"

"It does indeed, my love!"

She smiled back at him, all her love for him shining in her eyes. At last no barriers stood between them. Not William Steele Hardware. Not Thomas Kingsmill. Or Bryony Lodge with its dark secrets. She was going to marry Benedict in South Bersted church and live with him in the beautiful old house which had been home to her from the moment he had escorted her through its gates. Just as he had been her own true love from the first meeting of glances on a day long ago in Perbroke Square.